CHAINS

A SHORT STORY

UNHEARD

ANTHOLOGY

VOICES

CHAINS

A SHORT STORY

UNHEARD

ANTHOLOGY

VOICES

MARGŌ COLLECTIVE

CHAINS: UNHEARD VOICES

First published in 2018 by
MARGŌ COLLECTIVE
margocollective.com : hello@margocollective.com : @margocllctv

A catalogue card for this book is available from the British Library.

ISBN (pb): 978-1-9995-9090-1
ISBN (e): 978-1-9995-9091-8

Printed and bound in Great Britain by Clays, Bungay, Elcograf S.p.A.

INTRODUCTION

Over 100 years ago Muriel Matters and Helen Fox chained themselves to the grille of the Ladies' Gallery. This was one of the protests of the suffrage movement in the lead up to passing of Representation of the People act, a truly pivotal moment in history that changed the conversation in living rooms across society.

In the centenary year of women's right to vote we explore the concept of chains, both literal and metaphorical, examining the circumstances and experiences that continue to affect us—be it gender, age, race, sexuality, life experience or religion.

The following pieces are from writers across the globe who all connected with this concept. These are their stories.

CONTENTS

Dear Jenni,
Thanks for everything!
Hope you enjoy the story.
Love, Shyama x

EPILOGUE

Dear Sarah,

This is so hard to put into words and I don't suppose anything I say will convey my reasons properly. But I can't stay around, it's agony to remain. Every time I wake in the early hours I'm disappointed that I haven't died in the night. I know that sounds melodramatic and I know you will think that this is just me being my usual, attention-seeking, diva-self, but I just feel so unbearably tired.

Do you remember the superheroes we were obsessed with when we were kids? The twins next door got us into them, with their Top Trumps cards. You wanted to be Wonder Woman and my favourite was Silver Surfer—I thought he was brilliant; he looked like he was made out of mercury. He looked like nobody could touch him—that's what I loved about him. I didn't just admire him, I wanted to be him! I even told Aunt Linda that I wanted to be Silver Surfer when I grew up, do you remember? I really wanted his superhero powers; I wanted to fly, but what I really wanted was a force field; a protective dome. Girl in the bubble. I used to dream about rescuing my friends and you from burning buildings. I didn't realise that I was destined to be frozen in time. I thought that to become a hero, all you had to do was grow up, but nobody told me how hard that would be, just to grow up.

ō

There was a bubble playing around on Victoria's cracked lips, swelling and deflating like the chin on Poppy's toy bullfrog. As Vic's chest rose and fell, so too did the bubble expand and contract. It was maddening, Vic would have hated it if she'd known; she was such a clean freak, trying to deny any bodily functions, banning any toilet talk when we'd eat. She would have hated to be seen in such a vulnerable position.

"Mummy, shall I pop that bubble?" Poppy asked Sarah.

"No, darling, we mustn't touch anything."

"Auntie Vicki's not a thing, she's a human!" Poppy squeaked indignantly. A couple of the other patients and their visitors looked over.

"Shh, keep your voice down," Sarah hissed.

"But you said we shouldn't touch any*thing*, like Auntie Vicki is a thing," Poppy persisted.

"I just meant that it might be dangerous to touch any of the equipment and stuff and that we mustn't disturb Auntie Vicki," Sarah said, in a shouty kind of whisper.

"Is she asleep?" Poppy asked, kicking her foot against the bed, rhythmically.

"Sort of." Sarah replied, a catch in her throat, her hand stopping Poppy's foot.

ō

Deep below and beyond them, Vic floated in lukewarm water, beneath the surface, weeds above her. She could hear the echoes of her sister and her niece, the pitches of their voices, but not the words. A whale song, coming to her over the waves.

ō

Stuart came through the door at the same time as them.

"Daddy!" Poppy was ecstatic.

"Hello monkey!" He swung his daughter round in the hallway, knocking a couple of jackets off the overburdened coat hooks as he did so.

"How was Vic?" He asked.

"Oh, you know, no change," Sarah said, picking up the coats.

"Did you bring me anything, Daddy?" Poppy demanded.

"Might have."

Poppy bounced down and unzipped his bag.

"Whoa. Wait a minute Popsicle. Let me get in properly first."

Poppy was delighted with her sticker book and bag of giant chocolate buttons and ran into the living room with her spoils. They sat with their coffees and caught up, every now and then interrupted by Poppy, asking them which sticker they'd like, before placing one solemnly on one of their chests.

"Did you speak to the doctor?" Stu asked, cramming one of Poppy's sweets in his mouth.

"Not this time, I thought I'd go again tomorrow, on my own."

"OK, sure, I'll take Poppy to the park or something. Did your mum go and see her today?"

"No, she had her scan, she couldn't make it. I need to ring her, actually, see how it went. Christ, Stu, my family are falling apart at the seams!"

"Yeah, but with Victoria it's self inflicted."

She looked up at him sharply.

"I'm sorry but you know what I mean..."

ō

Do you remember that article we read? That horrible so-called guru urging everyone to 'Shut the fuck up' about their childhoods. Just get over it, move on. He actually had that as one of his mantras: 'Shut the fuck up!'

The thing is, even if you do shut up about it, even if you never talk about it at all, it's still there—poisoning everything you touch, it's still oozing through the concrete like toxic waste.

ō

"Who was that?" Stuart asked, as Sarah hung up the phone.

"Nihal."

"Nihal?"

"Yeah, he's back from France, visiting family, someone told him about Vic, he wants to go and see her."

"Do you think that's a good idea?"

"Dunno, maybe, maybe not."

"Will he bring his wife?"

"No, she's still in France."

"I see."

"She's 38 weeks pregnant; she can't travel."

"You don't think Nihal's visit might—"

"Might what?"

"I dunno, give Vic false hope or something."

"We don't even know if she's going to regain consciousness; I don't know about giving her false hope."

"Maybe he wants to see her before she… in case she…"

Unbidden, the image of the bubble of spit on Vic's mouth came to Sarah's mind, the world tipped sideways. She had to cling onto the kitchen counter to steady herself.

"Are you OK?" Stuart put his arm around her.

She nodded, she didn't have time to cry.

Breathe in—hello moment.

Breathe out—I am here.

ō

Do you remember the first time we did yoga—at the sports centre? And that horrible old bag told me that I stood with a squint? Do you remember that? I had a massive hangover and she said to me, "Do you know that you stand with a squint?" And she told you that you needed to exercise because you worked in an office. We went out and got full-fat lattes after that, do you remember? Christ, it put me off yoga for a lifetime, I felt like saying to her—I thought this was supposed to be relaxing!

I was always looking for something that would help but nothing seemed to. Yoga, mindfulness, CBT. I did try, Sarah. I guess that some things just can't be fixed.

ō

In bed, Stuart reached for Sarah. She turned away from him.

"I haven't seen you all week," he pleaded.

"I'm not in the mood."

He put his hand under her pyjama top and skimmed it over her breast, she pushed him away.

"Come on, it won't take long."

Thoughts of Nihal. Burst plum lips, Bambi eyes. That sudden wave of longing washing over her in a meeting—a tangible 3D wedge of desire. Could everyone else see it? Him carrying on as if there hadn't been an earthquake. All ridiculous, she'd probably been premenstrual, but after that she'd felt clumsy and awkward around him.

Then him and Vic hooking up. The thing about Vic was that she could be the most amazing, sparkling company, when she turned it on, she could make everything seem brighter and more colourful; whatever that magic ingredient was that some people had—charisma, energy, charm, she had it. But, she could also be, by her own admission, a moody bitch. She'd already dismissed all of Sarah's work colleagues as 'boring suits' and couldn't be bothered with them. If she ever came along with Sarah, to her work dos, she'd usually just spend the whole time looking at her phone. She'd even made a set of paper dolls for Poppy, once, colouring them in grey felt tip, telling the little girl that the paper dolls were Mummy's work friends. Then, to Sarah's horror, that night in The Crown, Vic and Nihal had hit it off, instantly. Moving away from the huddle blocking the bar and finding themselves at a little table in the corner of the pub. Nihal throwing his head back with laughter and Vic leaning in to touch his arm. Agony to watch.

"Your little sister is great!" Nihal said when he came over to get a drink.

"She's my older sister actually," Sarah said, but he'd turned his back on her already, to get the barman's attention and didn't hear her.

ō

I manage to fuck up everything that's good in my life. It was so good with Nihal, at the start. He was beautiful, wasn't he? Properly beautiful, 'handsome' wouldn't have done him justice. I think we all fancied him, even Mum! He really felt like my other half. I finally knew what people were going on about when they talked about other halves. It always makes me think of avocados. When you put us together, we slotted in like Lego.

I still think about him all the time; he's the first thing I think about when I wake up in the morning. I still dream about him. I drove him away. He couldn't cope with all my issues. We stopped having sex. I've never told anybody this but I couldn't even bear for him to watch me get undressed; it made me go all cold. Even though I loved him, it creeped me out. So, I don't blame him for walking away.

That guy in the Cedar Centre, with a face like a crumbling Madeira cake, "You've just got to move on with your life, Victoria, don't let them win."

The fuck he knew?

ō

Stuart had made pancakes with Poppy and was trying to stop their daughter pouring half a bottle of maple syrup onto hers, when Sarah came down the next morning.

"Oh, fluffy!" Poppy came over to her and stroked the arm of her angora jumper, leaving a snail trail of maple syrup in her wake.

"Poppy!" Sarah rubbed irritably at her arm with a baby wipe.

"You OK?" Stuart proffered the plate of pancakes towards her and she shook her head.

"Yeah, I suppose."

"What shall we do today Popsicle? Park?"

"Yeah! Can I bring my scooter?"

"Only if I get a go on it."

She left them laughing in the kitchen and went up to check on her phone which she'd left charging in the bedroom. There was a long message from Nihal, explaining apologetically that Celine had had a 'show' and he was flying back to Paris.

Give Vic my very best, he wrote. *I really hope she comes through all this!*

Sarah threw her phone down in disgust, even amidst all her worry and fear for Vic, she felt a little cheated. She unplugged her phone and grabbed her bag. She'd grab a coffee on the way, she just needed to be active now, moving.

She quickly kissed a very sticky Poppy goodbye, blew a kiss to Stu and ran out of the house.

ō

It hadn't been surprising that Vic had gone for Nihal, he'd been just her type, Sarah thought as she drove along the dual carriageway. Sensitive, arty, gently humorous, which was, slightly, if Sarah gave it due scrutiny, feminine in some way. Perhaps she didn't mean feminine but comfortable with his feminine side. Unassuming. Not Sarah's usual type at all but totally Vic's.

Stuart had once quipped that Vic's ideal man came from the 'Non-threatening Boys' magazine—a joke that he had taken from *The Simpsons,* meaning that she liked clean shaven, boyish men. Nothing too alpha.

She thought back to Nihal's text—'I really hope she comes through all this!' So do I mate, so do I! She's my big sister, my only sister. People used to think we were twins, even though we're three years apart. We used to put on our own plays when we were kids and perform them for our parents. She was a perfect mimic, could parrot someone's accent or mannerisms perfectly. She'd regale us with impersonations of old Mrs Vyse next door or of Aunt Linda, with her cod-posh voice. Whenever I read something funny, I used to think—I must remember to tell Vic that. She was a pain in the arse but she was the best. Why am I already thinking of her in the past tense? Sarah slammed her hand down on the steering wheel, hard.

ō

I wanted to protect you, Sarah, that's why I never told you about it. You were so pure and innocent. Why ruin two people's lives? That's what I thought. I knew you were safe because we'd all stopped going round there by then, so I knew I didn't need to warn you.

I see you now with your life all sorted out with Stuart and Poppy and everything, and I know I made the right decision but for me there's no getting away from it. I can't just 'get over it' or 'forget about the past' I just can't, I'm tied to it. I can't outrun it and I'm sick of trying. At least this way, you won't have to worry about me anymore, any of you.

Oh but Poppy, sis, she's so brilliant! She reminds me of you when you were little—same cheeky little grin, same incredible imagination. She's got some of Mum in her too, she's such a friendly, sociable little thing. I don't know if you realise how lucky you are to have her. I'll be sorry not to see her grow up, tell her that her Auntie Vicki loved her to the moon and back. Make sure you protect her, sis, let her know what's out there. When we were kids it was all 'don't talk to strangers' but most of the time it's not the strangers you have to worry about.

I never told you this, but when Poppy was born I cried my eyes out, I felt this real sense of loss. I think I was kind of grieving for what I could never have. I was happy for you of course, especially after what you and Stu had gone through with the miscarriages and stuff, but you having a baby symbolised this whole world that was cut off from me. That first time I held her, Sarah, it was as if she'd always been there, this perfect little being. I can still remember the weight of her in my arms and the warmth. And you know that I've never been one of those women who go gooey over babies, I just never got it, but with our little Poppy, I got it. Please let her know how much I loved her, how I was sorry not to say goodbye, christ, I'm crying so much I can barely see to write this. I think I'm going to leave it there.

I'm sorry if you think this is selfish of me but I'm just so tired.

Love, always, Vic

ō

The doctor had been cautiously optimistic—they'd seen 'signs', 'activity'. Sarah scanned Vic's face, to see if she could sense any change. Vic looked the same as she had yesterday though. Sarah unwrapped the note again, but felt disloyal looking at it in front of the other patients, even though, rationally, she knew they wouldn't really be able to read it from where they were, she still furtively stuffed it back into her bag.

She grabbed Vic's hand and squeezed it.

"You don't have to outrun your feelings, Vic, you just have to… you have to confront them." Sarah glanced around her nervously and scraped her chair closer to Vic's bed.

"I guess that's easy for me to say, when I'm not the one it happened to but… I've been reading about this and, you know, with counselling and stuff, you might start to feel better… The Cedar Centre wasn't proper therapy. You know that thing you said in the letter, about not liking Nihal watching you get undressed? That could be to do with suppressed memories, I've read about it. A therapist could help you deal with that, maybe." Her voice cracked. "Please don't leave me, Vic, I need you. Look, now who's being selfish, but I do need you, we all need you; me and Mum and Poppy. Please come back."

Was there a change? A ripple? Sarah squeezed Vic's hand tighter.

"Come back," she hissed. "You don't have to do this on your own."

ō

The voice in the ether again. A reed had been thrown down into the murky depths.

INCUBUS

On his deathbed, Polly's father, who was touching the frontiers of senility, told her that his biggest regret was spending so much time masturbating. In his childhood, teenage years, adulthood and even as recently as his sixtieth birthday, he'd liked nothing better than giving himself a bit of homemade entertainment, watching the people walk by through the blinds of his bedroom window as he did so, so he could see when his wife got home. She was there, too, in the hospital, and she looked at Polly as if to say *it's the dementia*. Polly believed her, but it didn't provide much relief.

ō

When she was a year old, Polly's parents took her on a holiday to the Pacific Northwest. They had family there, and it was supposed to be a clean place with fresh air, a lot of wildlife and cafés, so they didn't mind taking a baby on the ten-hour flight. On the third day they had left the pram by a bench to both go and peer into the marina. Her mother thought she'd seen an otter that turned out to be a piece of driftwood, and her father was enjoying teasing his wife, saying that she was seeing things. In that short minute, a seagull must have choked overhead, because a starfish—allegedly almost as big as baby Polly—fell from the sky and landed sunny side down in the pram. Polly's mother said she didn't remember screaming so much in her life. Grabbing it by one of its legs, she tossed it into the water without any thought for herself or it and slapped Polly's father ten or so times on the head. Polly was covered in blood and they thought at first the creature might have been poisonous or vicious, but the doctor later told them that it was neither. In fact, it was likely dead before it had even fallen. It must have been a big guy, they added, because it'd bruised the baby's body from head to toe, almost collapsed her year-old lung, broken her rib in three places and fractured her shoulder.

This was unimportant, however, because on performing regular checks they found that Polly had a disease that had gone unnoticed at birth. It meant the body failed to produce a certain enzyme that broke down a fatty substance with a long name. When they returned to England, the doctors told Polly's parents that she could live to thirty, maybe even forty, but it was rare for patients to make it further than that.

ō

Polly stayed home a lot, because more often than not she felt tired. On her sixteenth birthday her mother found a chest full of old photographs and said that Polly looked just like her grandmother. No one smiled in the photos and the sepia tone made them look like ghosts. For the most part, Polly's illness was under control, and since being diagnosed as a child, treatment in this area had advanced exponentially. Still, though, she was tired.

At eighteen Polly wasn't able to go to university and so studied a photography course online. The course was based in New York, so when she had a nine am deadline Polly could work on it until after lunchtime, thanks to the time difference. As good as this was, Polly often felt left out when they would talk on the forum about an exhibition that they should all go to or a trip they were taking. There was one other person on the course from overseas. They were learning photography to document the Civil War that ravaged their homeland, caused regular collateral damage and was likely to topple their long-standing dictator.

For most of her life Polly had suffered from poor sleep and as a result she had trained herself to sleep in short bursts, which meant her dreams were vivid and lifelike. The morning after the first time she'd tried alcohol, on the night of her sixteenth birthday, she woke up paralysed. Often her dreams contained malevolent creatures of some sort. Zombies were common, and she sometimes woke up with the smell of rotting flesh in her nostrils. When she woke up on this occasion, still drunk, early enough for it to be dark outside, she had the feeling that there was a little man sitting on her chest, holding her down with his weight, and not only that, but holding down her entire body to the point that all she could move were her eyes. Polly couldn't make a sound. She wanted to scream but it wouldn't come. Even her big toes stayed stubbornly stuck in place.

ō

He was only fifty-eight when he was diagnosed with dementia, but Polly's father deteriorated quickly. It was not a gradual decline, but rather a problem that worsened his mind in steps. One day he would be coping well and the next he would tumble suddenly further into darkness. Early morning, after one of these steps, he had wandered outside. Not far down the road was a large estate (worth over five million pounds, so the rumour was) which Polly's father had often remarked upon, as its grounds were filled with flowers and exotic plants, enough to warrant a gardener who worked every day except Sunday. In his confusion, Polly's father had scaled the low wall and entered the vast garden, brushing through flower patches and following the running water which turned from a stream to a moat and then back again. The rich South-African owner was soon told about the intruder, but knew Polly's father well and so the adventure did not end on bad terms. Not an hour passed before, back at home, he complained about feeling ill. The pain grew more severe, so Polly and her mother took him to the hospital, and it was then that he started to tell her about his regret at masturbating his youth away.

He died of multiple organ failure. Apparently the South-African had been cultivating aconitum, or Devil's Helmet, and Polly's father had brushed past the plant during his walk.

ō

When Polly was twenty-five she went into hospital herself. She had been staying in the Lake District, freelancing for a walking-tour company who needed photographs for their promotional magazine, when she fainted and had to travel back home to be seen by her doctor. She didn't leave the hospital as quickly as she had in previous visits, as the pain had become worse and the fatigue was, for the time being, keeping her in bed. This was part of her condition, so not entirely unexpected. It worried her though, as the list of eventual symptoms checked themselves off as she grew older. Towards the end of their lives, apparently, patients of her condition could suffer with dementia. Her father's hadn't been connected in any way, but Polly couldn't help wonder at the coincidence and fear becoming the shell he had.

Just before he had died, as well as masturbation, Polly's father had talked incessantly about his family history. He couldn't remember anyone suffering from Polly's disease, but then they hadn't been a close family. He reminisced about the games he and his cousins had played as children and the movies he had seen with her mother. His muffled way of speaking echoed around Polly's mind as she drifted in and out of sleep, trying in vain to get comfortable in the hospital bed. Her mother was sat by the bedside holding her hand.

He had said, just before drifting away himself, "Polly, you were the best thing that happened to me. There's nothing I can think of that's more worthwhile in life than just carrying it on, you know. Passing the genes. I'm glad I masturbated as much as I did, because it was obviously just the right amount to make sure you were front of the queue when you were."

It was a nice sentiment, even though he'd never have dreamed of speaking like that while in his regular mind. All Polly could think of was the image of her father grunting over a tissue.

ō

She woke up in the middle of the night, machines beeping around her, elderly patients coughing in the distance. The nurse yawned at her desk. Polly could spy on her through the gap in the curtain, usually, but tonight she found she couldn't move again. The little man, the demon, was back on her chest, except she did not feel the same panic as the times before. The demon was the same as he had always been, but this time she felt settled in its familiarity, and besides, he did not have the same malicious look on him as usual. His eyes were sad and his mouth glum. Distracted, was how he looked. It didn't affect how effectively he had her pinned to the mattress, but for the first time it seemed fine by her. In his growl, he said, "Would you rather go consecutively or counter-consecutively?"

Polly couldn't answer and he realised his mistake, so just began.

"The most recent was your grandmother, who went at the age of eighty-nine after a tumble in the street. A head injury turned to a hospital trip. Then, an infection. She had three children, one of which had one child, another two children and the last two also. Before her was your great-grandmother, who was on an aeroplane when it happened on her seventy-sixth birthday. She was old, but they did not know she had a weak heart until the turbulence upset her and she ran out of breath before they could land. She had smoked her entire life, and they think the smoke circling the cabin hurried her end along. It was a different time. She had four children, your grandmother, a boy and two more girls. They had six children between them. Her mother was your great-great, and she died, I'm not joking, by being struck in the head by a stray cricket ball, aged forty-one. Six children. Your great-times-three was a remarkable woman. She'd worked in the factories as a child and her lungs had filled with black. She lived to fifty-five and had seven children. She was known around the town for causing fights in the street when people noted how scrawny and owlish she looked. She died coughing blood into her open palms. Her mother died in childbirth, aged twenty-two. In the eighteenth century you had a relation who was six-foot tall and adept at hunting. She lived into her forties, until she fell from a horse. She survived two days on willpower alone before succumbing to internal bleeding brought on by a severe break in her ribs. In the seventh generation back, your great-times-six could not read and had had no education to speak of. She was a painter and died age thirty-three, a long life, relatively. She went in her sleep. No one knew why.

In seventeen-thirty-three, the church bells rang so often that they were deemed to be a public nuisance and your great-times-seven did her bit by causing them to ring in the days after fever took her, age thirty. She had four children before that, none of whom made it past thirty themselves, for one reason or another. Her mother died at twenty-seven, and she had lived a life dedicated to the pursuit of pleasure, or, in the minds of her contemporaries, and indeed those who had her killed, the pursuit of perversity. She wasn't legally killed, mind you, but some, especially once you get back to the beginning to the eighteenth century, refused to relinquish their freedom to punish others to the state. Allegedly, she had sex with thirty-two different men. Quite a feat for a woman of her time. Great-times-nine did not work, but instead cared for her five children. She made a great stew and died on her tenth wedding anniversary walking into the sea on a windy night."

The doctors had told Polly she was experiencing pain in her bones and that it would likely get worse. It might have been psychological, but when they said that she found she could feel the bones themselves. Creaking and splintering somewhere inside her.

"There are forty-five more generations to go until we get to the Roman Empire. Four-hundred-and-eighty until we reach what we consider the start of *civilisation*. Shall I go on?"

Polly thought about it, but said *no* by scrunching her eyes shut. There didn't seem much point.

"Skip to thirty-five generations. We're in the second century. She died of malnutrition. Seven children. Starved her to death."

She managed to move her little finger, just a twitch. Usually this broke the spell of paralysis, but still the demon pinned her down.

"One-hundred back. Dead at twenty-three, three children. Five-hundred back. Three children too, dead at eighteen, trauma to the head. But, then, these are cheating somewhat. Everyone's related to everyone once we get this far back. Everyone has traces of everyone else."

She balled her hand into a fist and the rest of her body tensed and twitched. The demon disappeared and the dream state dissipated into reality again. The machines around her beeped and coughed.

ō

There had been boyfriends, both serious and temporary. Her favourite had been Bruno. A strange name for a skinny white kid from Yorkshire, but he suited it. He had been five years older than Polly and worried a lot about the direction his life was going, because by age twenty-two his mother and father had been married and were expecting a baby, and what was he doing? He was an only child and his parents were pushy. When she was seventeen, Bruno asked Polly if she would consider eloping, getting married, having children, it would be crazy, exciting, spontaneous, how about it? She had doctor's appointments, however. Come on, it's not like you have much time to waste finding someone else, he said, and knew he'd said something stupid, because he dropped it after that. That was eight years ago.

He went to medical school and was probably married by now.

ō

It's so difficult to distinguish between dreams and reality sometimes. And it can be much worse than that. It can be difficult, also, to distinguish between two simultaneous realities. Namely, the present and the future, or the present and the past or even two potential futures. I am alive, I am going to die. I am going home to have dinner with my family, I am never going to leave this hospital bed. One day I will get married and have children, one day I will disappear into the dirt and become it, one and the same.

ō

The plane touched down at JFK and already Polly could feel the East Coast's summer heat making her forehead sweat. Passengers were taking their bags down, though the seatbelt signal was still lit up, and being on the aisle seat, Polly found herself forced into the crowd, pushed forwards and heading towards the exit.

It was night-time and the lights in the plane flickered on and off. It would have made a good photograph, that scene, because the seats were all empty, but the aisle was full of people jostling for space, hot and bothered, in all states of disarray. Outside the vehicles that transported luggage and directed pilots beeped and revved. The pulsing lights on the runway reminded her of monitors by hospital bedsides. Distant city lights replaced them as she took the AirTrain to the station. As she walked from the train into the city and around the streets, looking up at the buildings and squinting at the pulsing colours of the billboards, it seemed like a dream. Taking out her camera, she took shots of people with the shutter speed on low so that it looked as if they were ghosts leaving a trail of themselves throughout the city, being constantly followed by a recent snapshot of their existence, or constantly leaving themselves behind, their tail chasing them.

Soon everyone started to take on this form. Multiple versions of everyone stretched back for miles, the past seemed disconnected from the present, imprinted on time as if it simply refused to let go. But then, the present people kept walking, leaving more versions of themselves behind, moving quicker and quicker as if they knew what was back there and couldn't bear to think of it.

ō

In the hotel Polly listened to the taxi cabs passing by and felt her eyelids drooping and her mind dulling. She couldn't tell if she was asleep or awake. She moved her little finger but remembered that she wasn't paralysed, only confused. Each time a car passed by the light slipped through the break in the curtains and lit up the room, and distant sirens sounded like malfunctioning heart monitors. The jet lag made Polly feel as if she was already asleep and only dreaming she was here, in this city, finally visiting her friends from the course. Her bones still ached and she tossed and turned. The beeping grew louder and the lights flickered again. It didn't seem real.

LIKING, LUMPING, AND THE FANCY WOMAN

Roddy was woken by the sound of his mother talking to someone in the other room but as soon as he was awake all he could think was: today is when it will happen.

To find out what it would be like, he had thrown himself into holly bushes, rolling around in them, and the prickles didn't make him bleed and didn't even hurt, not really. But that did not make the squeezed feeling in his tummy, as he lay in bed, go away.

The squeezed feeling was a bit less when he thought how being thrown in the holly hedge happens to *all* the boys, not just him, after you're seven and have to go down the steps and play in the Lower Playground.

But after he had been thrown in the holly hedge he would not be who he now was. His inside would have gone.

The squeezed feeling came back even worse.

He wished he could wear long trousers for it, but they weren't allowed until you went to the secondary school, where they called you by your surname and he would just be Dunlop, not Roddy. Anyway, his mother couldn't afford long trousers.

When she came into the bedroom she just sat on the bed. She didn't start to get him up. After a while she cried.

"Don't cry," Roddy said it quietly. That might mean she was not really crying.

"I'm not crying," she said, in the bright voice that he liked. It felt like something strong holding him up. "I must have got something in my eye, I expect. Now, you don't want to be late the first day school starts back and you going up into a new class!"

But still she sat on the bed.

Then she said, "Mr Scobie came up early to tell me we've got to leave here. We've to go today. We'll have to go back to Gran and Grandad's. Mr Scobie said he was ever so sorry and would give us back our rent. That was nice of him. It's important to be nice, Roddy."

Roddy said, "I don't like Gran for making us go back and live with her."

"No, Roddy, it's not Gran making us go back. You see, there's someone who can pay Mr Scobie a lot more rent than I can afford. We mustn't complain. It's his house and he can do what he likes with it. He doesn't have to let us live here."

"If I had a house I'd let people who can't afford the rent live here."

"Like you let Donald Russell play with your toys," she said, in the telling-him-off voice that meant the opposite of what she said. Yesterday he'd shown his Bayko Building Set to Donald Russell down the road. He'd only *shown* it, but Donald Russell had started playing with it, putting rods in the base to build a house, banging them with bits of wall that slotted into the rods, and Roddy had pushed Donald Russell and Donald Russell's mother had complained to Roddy's mother.

Her bright voice came back. "Perhaps when we've been back at Gran's for a bit we can afford somewhere nicer. Not somewhere still with bomb damage. You'd think old Scobie'd have done something about it all these years after the war. Somewhere with an Osokool so the milk won't go off. Some houses have fridges."

"Is his fancy woman going to live here?" Roddy said, to show he was sharp.

"Her in these rooms!" She looked around at the stove and the wobbly little table and the armchair which pulled out to be her bed. It was like she was picturing the fancy woman there. Then she smiled. "You're too young to be thinking about fancy women." He liked her saying that, because saying it meant that really he was *not* too young. He was becoming a big boy.

But becoming a big boy meant he wasn't allowed to play in the Girls' and Infants' Playground anymore and had to go and play with the big boys in the Lower Playground and be thrown in the holly hedge.

Anyway, it was his mother who'd told him about fancy women. One night when Mrs Scobie was in hospital they'd heard a lady laughing a lot in the house below. Each laugh started with a high screech and then fell down into a giggle. His mother stood with her ear to the door, telling him to shush, and then she opened it and crept down the narrow wooden stairs, all closed in, that led to the landing of Mr Scobie's house.

After a while her footsteps came hurrying back up and she shut the door. She said—but not really to Roddy—"Old Scobie's found a fancy woman!" Then she laughed and laughed, screwing up her face.

Roddy laughed back. "Old Scobie's found a fancy woman!"

Her voice changed. "We mustn't think that, Roddy. I expect it's just someone Mrs Scobie asked to come in and do cleaning and things while she's in hospital. I expect I was mistaken, what I heard. I always am mistaken. And don't you go mentioning it to Mrs Scobie. You never gain anything in life by telling tales."

It would be telling tales if he told his mother he would be thrown in the holly hedge when he went back to school.

She said, "It would upset Mrs Scobie and she's always nice to you."

Yes, Mrs Scobie was nice. But she was posh and didn't like fun, so she would never do the cancan.

"It would be a lie, I'm sure it would, saying he's got—a woman like that. Telling lies is wrong, Roddy."

"Why?" But Roddy had said it in the voice in which he would ask her to tell a favourite bedtime story.

She had said, "You feel bad in yourself if you tell lies. Now, it's time for bed."

ō

Today, the day of the holly hedge, it was hard to eat his

breakfast because of the squeezed feeling in his tummy and because the milk for his porridge was nearly off. But if he left it, his mother would ask what was wrong.

"My, you're slow this morning. And I've got to get on with moving us back to Gran's. I'll have to lose a day's work. I just hope I don't lose my job, and all."

"If you lose your job, you could be Mr Scobie's fancy woman again."

He laughed because he did not know what else to do about the look she had turned on him, a look in which he wasn't Roddy.

"Don't you *ever* say that again." In the voice, there was only anger, not his mother. He was where he would be when he was thrown in the holly hedge. "Or I'll leave you with Gran and run away. Me his fancy woman!" To some-one else she said, "I might as well have, for all..."

Roddy started crying. "You *were*. His fancy woman. You did cleaning for him and Mrs Scobie when we came here from Gran's, before the job at International Stores."

She looked at him and he was Roddy again. She burst out laughing. "A fancy woman isn't someone who does cleaning."

"What is it?"

"You'll find out when you're older."

But he was older. He was going to be thrown into the holly hedge.

She said, "A fancy woman is someone a man treats like she's his wife but she isn't and it's wrong."

He did not want to hear anymore about what a fancy

woman was, for it must be not nice. He put the strap of his new satchel over his head. It was a real leather one, a present from Gran and Grandad, with a lovely new-leather smell in its pale rough inside. He started to cry again. "I want to still live here. Not his fancy woman. It's lovely here."

"Lovely?—The skylight leaking and this old lino I keep tripping over? And lugging every drop of water for cooking up those stairs? And at Gran's I won't have to sleep on that filthy old armchair, Roddy." In her voice she was asking him to understand like a big boy would.

"I've got an idea." He put on the look people had in comics when they had a bright idea. She looked round from piling up the breakfast dishes. She seemed to believe he really could tell her how to put everything right. "Tell Mr Scobie he's got to let us stay else we'll tell Mrs Scobie he has a fancy woman to treat like his wife and it's wrong."

"Oh, no, Roddy." But he thought she wanted to do what he said.

"No, Roddy." Her stern voice. "That's not a nice thing to do. You don't get anywhere in life by threatening people. It's what they call blackmail. You can be put in prison for blackmail. Now promise me you won't say that to Mr Scobie."

"Promise."

"And promises have to be kept, so mind you keep it. Just because some men break promises… If you're a good person and do what's right, you never know what's round the corner. I expect we'll find a nicer place and say, 'We'd never be here if we hadn't had to leave Mr Scobie's.'"

"The Queen's got the sword of justice they gave her at the Coronation and she's got to help people." At school, all the children had learned about the Coronation ceremony and been taken to see *A Queen is Crowned* at the pictures. "She'll let us stay."

"The Queen wouldn't take any notice of us, Roddy. We've got to like it or lump it, what people do to us. So we'd better start liking it."

Roddy said, "Lump it," and put his fists up his jumper so that it looked like he had a bust. "Lumps," he said.

This was naughty, but his mother only smiled, looking sad. "Time for school."

"Cancan?"

He thought she was going to tell him he was naughty to ask, but suddenly she laughed and held out her dress and started kicking up her legs, and Roddy kicked up his legs, too, satchel slapping against his side, and as they danced—not moving from the spot because the kitchen was too small to move around in—Roddy la-la'd the cancan tune and his mother joined in: la-la-la-la, la-la-la-la, la-la-la-la, la-la-LAAH... As he danced he saw for the first time that the kitchen and his little bedroom, where even he couldn't stand up on one side because the ceiling was so low, were really all one room with a wall put in.

"Now, school!" She followed him down the little shut-in stairs, carrying dishes she would later wash in the top bathroom. Then they went side by side down Mr Scobie's wide stairs with the thick green carpet. Near the front door, there he was. Roddy's mother said, "Just seeing Roddy off to school, Mr Scobie, then I'll start packing up our things." She said it as if they were leaving their home to be nice to Mr Scobie.

Mr Scobie smiled at Roddy, but it was not a nice smile. The top of his head was bald. He looked like Scrooge in the film they'd seen at the pictures. His eyes never moved when he looked at you. "Are you going to get beaten? Schools give boys beatings."

Roddy's mother had told him Mr Scobie had been to a posh school called Rugby where you didn't go home every day after school. You lived there, and it was like *Tom Brown's School Days*, and there were beatings. Being beaten at Rugby, Roddy thought, would be like being thrown in the holly hedge. He would be being beaten but it would be being done to someone who wasn't Roddy any more. "You should be beaten, because you do wrong things, like how you treat your wife."

"Roddy!" Her voice told him that he had done something awful. He wondered if God would strike him dead, like God did to a man for touching the Ark of the Covenant in *David and Bathsheba*, that they'd seen at the pictures. "I'm ashamed of you, speaking to Mr Scobie like that. Say you're sorry."

"That's why boys deserve to be beaten. They're cheeky." Mr Scobie raised his arm as if to thrash Roddy with an invisible stick.

"Sorry." Roddy laughed, to show that what he'd said

had only been in fun, but he started the laugh with a high screech and made it fall down into a giggle, like the woman's they'd heard.

He did it again.

In the silence he did it a third time.

"I'm afraid my husband has a business appointment and will be unable to help you move your things with the car, Miss—Mrs Dunlop." Suddenly Mrs Scobie was there. It was the first time Roddy had seen her since her operation, but she did not look any different. She was very tall and had a wide flat stomach which it would be nice to lean up against. She smiled down at Roddy. "And Roddy's things, too, of course. Unless he'd like to stay and be *my* little boy."

"A business appointment, yes," said Mr Scobie, nodding.

"Oh, it's no trouble, it'll only take a couple of bus rides, we haven't got much. Luckily it was a furnished flat." She said the last bit like telling Mr Scobie something he didn't already know.

Mrs Scobie said to Roddy, "Wait there," and went off, and came back with a purse. "Buy yourself something to remind you of your friend Mrs Scobie." She handed him two half-crowns.

"Mum! I can get the car pulling a caravan in Holbrook's." Mrs Scobie couldn't be a friend because she was a grown-up, but he did not say this.

"What do you say, Roddy?"

"Thank you, Mrs Scobie. And when I get it I will let other children play with it, like Donald Russell, because he is poor and doesn't have nice toys." He turned to Mr Scobie. "If you've got things that are yours you should let people live there and play with them."

"What a nice thing to say, Roddy!" said Mrs Scobie. And she took a third half-crown from her purse and gave it to him as though no one else could see her doing it and this was a secret extra present.

His mother said he might lose the half-crowns at school. Did she know about being thrown in the holly hedge and take them so they wouldn't fall out of his pocket? The squeezed feeling came back but then he thought: perhaps being thrown in the holly hedge, that being done to me, will help Mummy.

"Remember you go home to Gran's when you go home tonight," she called as he went down the road and she waved from the doorsteps as she always did.

In the Upper Playground he wondered whether to stay there. He could tell the teacher he had forgotten that now he had to play in the Lower Playground. But that would be a lie and telling lies was wrong and he would feel bad inside.

Then Pam Cheve, whose hair was all frizzy, who was always whispering with people and saying she knew a secret, said, "If you don't play in the Lower Playground the teachers make you wear a dress."

"You're a fancy woman," he said back.

She started pointing and shouting. "He's going to wear a dre—ess!"

Pam Cheve did not touch him but it felt like he was

being pushed to the steps and then down them. Roddy decided he would not let Donald Russell play with the car pulling a caravan.

The holly hedge was all across the bottom end of the Lower Playground. A game of football was going on; the boys playing it must be the nice ones. But some boys were standing at the foot of the steps, looking at him with smiles that were not nice smiles. One of them, Timothy Martin, lived near Roddy's Gran's. Roddy had played with him in the street but now he behaved as if he didn't know Roddy. He said, "He's another one going up."

Suddenly Roddy took off running and was down the steps and through the gang before they could grab him. He headed straight for the holly hedge. The gang chased him, shouting "Get him" and "Throw him in!"

He ran full pelt into the holly hedge, pressing himself into its deep inside, rolling himself this way and that. He called out, "This is lovely, I *like* being in the holly hedge."

The gang watched. Timothy Martin said, "No, he's got to be *thrown*. You can't just *go* in the holly hedge."

Roddy remembered the song about being beside the seaside and sang out, "Oh, I do like to be in the holly hedge," and he made movements with his arms like someone swimming, though actually he couldn't swim.

Someone said, "Well, he's in there, so... Look, there's another one." The gang rushed up the playground to where another little boy, Roger Bradley, was coming down the steps, looking scared. Roddy wished he could tell him the secret of how to prevent being thrown in the holly hedge.

GARGOYLE

After he was captured, they threw him into an underground cell in the graveyard prison, closed the door shut, and left him there like a corpse on the floor of a morgue. They shut him off from the world, shut the world off from him. He was sure that those on the outside would soon forget him, forget that he had once lived amongst them. The darkness threw a veil over him till his past drifted further away, till it became a hazy distant dream and he could no longer remember why he was there in this dungeon, this black hole. The winter sunk into the underground and left his body shivering on the floor. Frostbite brushed the tip of his little finger and turned it black, as if the darkness had seeped into his skin. Days, nights passed, till he could no longer tell them apart, till they coalesced into one... into daynights... Time was a rubber band that stretched to fill the endless hours and minutes. Then snapped back to a singular point with a sting.

The endless hours and minutes of his daynights were interrupted only by the clap of boots down the stairs and in the corridor beyond the cells. At times, when the guards marched past his cell, he glimpsed a sliver of their torch-light through the slot in the door, the light like a will-o'-

the-wisp in the forest, before the darkness snatched it away. Then, one daynight, the boots stopped in front of his cell. A guard crouched down and shone his torchlight through the slot in the door of his cell. That ray of torchlight was like the gaze of a basilisk; he turned to stone, transfixed. The torchlight roamed over him, his face a gargoyle's—his lips and the bridge of his nose swollen, his cheeks puffed out from their blows, his eyes sunk in their hollows, irises shrinking from the light. The torchlight lingered over his face, then roamed over the rest of his body, drew away when it was convinced that he was still alive. The guard slid a plate of food and a styrofoam cup of water through the slot. His fingertips traced over the food on the plate and knew what it was, a slice of black bread and half an apple—rotten from the softness of its skin. But he hadn't eaten in daynights, and his hunger was clamouring at his insides. His fingertips tore the bread to pieces. It was sour in his mouth, but he didn't care, washed it down with a sip of water afterwards. He ate the rotting fruit with the rest of the bread, down to the core. When he was done, he slid the plate out of the slot into the corridor beyond the door. He lay back down on the floor, his stomach twisting into knots, quivering. Within an hour, he was crouched over the small bucket in the corner, relieving his bowels, liquid shit leaving traces on his skin.

He washed himself with the quarter cup of water in the styrofoam cup that he had saved. But he did not feel clean afterwards, traces of shit clinging to skin, to hair. That daynight, he did not say his prayers in his unclean, wretched state. His prayers had been his salvation in the underground, but now, even that was out of reach. He was ashamed of his own body, a revulsion that grew each time he squatted over the bucket in the corner, till he imagined he would have whittled his own skin if he had a knife in his reach, cut himself down to the bone. As it was, his constant hunger whittled away his muscles, left him withered, ragged. Daynights passed. The guards stopped in front of his cell, pulled him out and dragged him up the stairs to the interrogation room. The darkness of the underground had turned him pale, colourless—a ghost of the graveyard prison. He stared through his burning, sleepless eyes at the CIA agent who sat behind the metal table, his face covered by a black mask, his handgun on the table between them. He thought of how the masked man was a mirror to his own hooded self, even though the guards had taken off his hood in the interrogation room. He saw that in the hole cut out in the mask around the lips, he had week old stubble. It gave him a more sinister look, as if his lips were strung with barbed wire. And in the holes cut above, his eyes were still, like black marbles on white chalk.

"Assalaam aley-kum," the agent greeted him, a familiarity in his tone. "How are you, Ismail?" he asked, his American voice drawn out, yet sharp. Ismail stared back at him, his eyes vacant. In his hand the agent held a gilt edged book with a green cover. Ismail recognised it as the holy book, the Quran. The agent walked around the table towards him and offered the holy book to him. "I want you to place your hand over this book before you answer my questions, so I know that you speak the truth," he said. But Ismail turned away, kept his hands behind him: how could he explain that he would not touch the holy book in his unclean state. When the CIA agent returned to the table, all he said was, "I don't want to listen to your fuckin' lies." He opened up the holy book in his hand, the English copy, turned the gilt-edged pages and read a passage aloud:

To Allah belongs all that is in the heavens and on earth. Whether you show what is in your minds or conceal it, Allah calls you to account for it. He forgives whom He pleases, and punishes whom He pleases. For Allah has power over all things.

He returned to the book, and kept on reading, not waiting for the terp to translate. Ismail rocked himself on the floor, turned his face to the side so he would not be forced to listen to the words of the book in his unclean state, to listen to the mocking voice. He kept his anger in abeyance, till it erupted within him. He pulled at the chains around his ankles and dragged himself towards the table, screamed so that he would drown out the words of the agent. The guard at the door was upon him in an instant, pinning his neck to the floor with his rifle. The black cloth that covered the guard's lips quivered as he breathed, and his eyes—the only part of his face that was visible—betrayed no flicker of emotion. In that moment, with the guard's rifle pressed hard against his throat, throttling him, Ismail decided that he would not answer any more of their questions in the interrogation room, that his silence would be his defiance.

The agent pulled the chair from behind the table towards Ismail. With the help of the guard, hc lifted Ismail off the floor and sat him down on the chair. He tied his hands to the back of the chair, while his ankles remained chained to the bolt on the floor. The guard held his neck while the agent pulled the black hood over Ismail's face and tightened the drawstring. They beheld the contours of his gargoyle face beneath the black cloth of the hood. Ismail twisted his face to the side till he found an air pocket that let him breathe easier inside the hood. They left him alone in the interrogation room, hooded and chained. The hood was like a black mirror held up before his eyes, turning him inward.

As Ismail sat in the chair, he thought how the world of the outside—the green hills and valleys of his youth, the sun and the moon, the stars at night—were not his anymore. His world was interior, the world of memories, of dreams, of fears known and unknown. He thought of that night when he lay on his floor, alone, his brother gone. Dead. The room empty, bereft, a hole within it that only the darkness could fill. He lay there awake, looking up, the ceiling like a sky without stars, without the moon, without hope. He reached across to the other side of the bed: it was empty and cold, and that coldness crept into him. He shivered, then broke into sobs, his little body trembling, shaking the tears out of him, which he wiped with the palm of his hands. As he sat strapped on the chair, hooded and chained, the cold fear of that long ago night burgeoned within him. His ragged body trembled. He pushed back against the chair and rocked himself harder and harder till both he and the chair fell to the ground. When the agent and the guard returned to the interrogation room, they found him lying on the floor, still strapped to the chair, the black hood over his face wet with his drool.

ō

The guards marched him down the underground corridor of cells, to the room at the end with the odour of rot on its walls. They raised his hands above his head and tied his wrists to the rod on the wall, shackled his feet to the bolt on the floor. This was his punishment for his silence, they said. He begged them for relief: were they not his fellow Afghans? Were they not his brother Muslims? But the guards turned their backs on him and left him there, hanging from the wall. He cursed them: that Allah was watching, that Allah would punish them for their sins. He listened to the sound of their boots fade till it was all quiet in the graveyard prison and he was left with his own ghosts. Feeling drained away from his limbs till his body turned numb, a husk of skin suspended between life and death. He knew that he could not bear this pain, this feeling that his body was sinking, as if into quicksand.

Like his body, he felt his mind too slipping from its tethers. The room filled with visions, hallucinations. He heard voices around him and he could not tell if there were others in the room or if they were disembodied voices rising out of the walls. He heard the voice of the CIA agent asking him the same questions as in the interrogation room—the questions repeated over and over till he screamed to drown them out. He hallucinated that hands were reaching out from the walls, pulling his limbs, tearing him apart, wrenching his heart from his ribs. And just before he lost consciousness and blacked out, he had a vision: that Death had raised its skeletal hands from the floor and grasped his ankles, that it was pulling him down into its subterranean crypt.

ō

The guards took him back to his cell. He lay in the void, the weight of its emptiness crushing him. His chest quivered and he broke into sobs.

"*Qui êtes-vous? Qui êtes-vous?*"

A voice from the other side of the wall called to him. He pushed his body off the floor and sat up, wondered if it was real or just another disembodied voice in the wall. Still, he was glad to hear it, even though he did not understand the words. He coughed, just to show that he was there, awake, listening.

"*Je m'appelle Abdel Aziz,*" the voice continued. "*Je suis algérien.*"

He understood that the man on the other side of the wall had spoken his name, no longer a ghost, an unknown. He cupped his hands around his mouth and put his lips to the wall.

"Ismail," he said, speaking aloud his name.

"*Ismail,*" the voice on the other side echoed.

He was pleased that someone else would know his name, that he would not simply disappear from this earth as if he had never lived. They called out the names of their families to each other, so that they too would not forget. Over many daynights, during lulls when the underground was quiet, when the boots were no longer marching outside their doors, they carried on a conversation, each in their own tongues, not understanding the other's words, but discerning meaning through tone and inflection and voice. They knew that if they stopped their conversation, they would each sink deeper into the abyss.

And when the voice on the other side fell silent, he spoke to the walls, and the walls spoke back to him, voices from his past, voices that were real and imagined. One daynight, as he lay on the floor, he heard the walls echo his own screams. He saw a vision of himself on the floor of the interrogation room. The Americans were standing around him, crowding him, beating him on his legs, on his hands, with baseball bats, the sound of their bats against his bones like a crackling flame. He cried out in pain, till he lay there on the floor, still, inert. The walls echoed his cries in his underground cell. He reached down and ran the tips of his fingers over his shins and calves, but the skin was smooth, with no lumps or bruises. He could not tell whether what he had seen was real or not.

And when even the walls fell silent, he spoke to the dark, his tongue like the tip of a knife, carving words into air, the words hovering over his lips in a cloud of moisture, weightless. He knew that as long as he could draw upon the skein of words, give them shape, speak them out loud—then at least in mind, if not in body, he was still human, and not animal.

And when even he fell silent and drifted off to sleep, he dreamed that the walls of his cell were closing in on him, till they enclosed him in a wooden coffin in this graveyard prison.

And in his dream, lying in his enclosed coffin, he whispered to himself: "better death than this, better death than this life."

ANCHOR

"Where have you been hiding yourself all this time?"

You balk at the question, stop, don't speak, then let your tongue deal out pleasantries while your brain seethes. It's been, what? Six years? Six years, yeah, without a single rattle, but now… now you hear it again.

He speaks with a slickness he's developed since then. You chuckle at his jokes, make sure not to laugh too hard, make sure you don't slip. Don't let the old words, the love words, don't let them slip past the teeth, cage them in, keep them deep inside. The pet names that work like full stops, that beg for use again. His hair has changed, grey now, silver, dignified. Yours has not, is not. Ratty. That's the word. Ratty. His eyes are harsher, yours are softer, filled with tears. You excuse yourself as you see his new partner start to walk over and the metal between you and him starts to shake. You don't want to be introduced to her, you've seen her before, stalked her, Facebooked her, seen all their holiday photos. You wonder, briefly, if they have seen yours. Seen those photos of you alone, stood slightly tense in front of monuments while you trusted strangers not to run, not to just take off with the camera and your photographic evidence that—yes—you are still alive. You are functioning. You are.

The barman comes over, looks puzzled when you order, but gets you that triple. Around you, people chatter with all the genteel aplomb of those desperate to make small talk. Caged comments, don't give too much away, but get all the info you can, all affection and soothing, sorrows and forced tears. The gin is cheap, burns, but it's fine. You've been fingering your phone while you drink, desperate to feel a buzz, a vibration, anything. You take the sleek sheet of touchscreen black out of your pocket and, in the reflection, catch a glimpse of him and her behind you, off talking to themselves. And, worse, the link forming clearer and clearer, out your back and snaking towards him. You switch the camera to forward facing and take a photo of them over your shoulder, then finish your drink. He is smiling, laughing, looks trim. His hand on her waist, where your scars are. You finish your drink and get another. Doesn't burn so much.

It's his suit. You know it, you know it. You pull out your phone and look at the lock screen background, where he and the new girlfriend stand, her hand on his waist. On his waist. But the suit he's wearing, the black suit, the trim suit, it must be that. Same suit as in the shop. You stand on your tiptoes, try to place your reflection within the borders of the suit, your neck in the collar, arms in the sleeves, but you can't quite seem to match up. You look again at the photo, catch her blurred pixel eye looking at you, at the camera. She's looking at you. She's looking. A rattle of the chain behind you, that runs through your body, trailing off somewhere into the city where he… where he…

You remember what you forgot to do this morning. You stand there in the street thinking, wondering, wondering if this is the right decision. You walk into the shop, keep your head down, down, eyes down. The price is right. You try it on, what's the harm? Feel the expensive fabric stutter over the scars on your arms, but that's nothing new. The rest feels good, fits fine. Reduced, floor copy, recently returned. Is it his? You open the lining, sniff for his aftershave, but surely they would have washed it. You try to imagine what it would be like to wear his suit, what it would be like to be there. You imagine finding a silver hair, or imagine holding it. You do find it, pluck it, hold it up to the mirror and look at him staring back at you, but with your ratty hair. You take the hair, place it along your fringe, press it into the hairline but it won't stick. The woman outside the changing room doors asks if you're okay, but you take a nail, ragged from this morning's biting, and dig it into the skin, dig and dig, until you feel something part and pop.

That's my girl, he says, from the mirror. *That's my girl.*

You feel blood pass the nail, but the hair is in. You feel it take root, grow in, draw in.

My girl, you're so beautiful, if only you'd try.

The tape is tight, but it needs to be, doesn't it? You peel it off slowly in the bathroom, unwind it for days until you're stood naked in front of the mirror. Your phone is on the sink, just below the mirror. You've zoomed in the image until it's just him. You don't like her eyes looking at you like that, like she knows. She knows. The tape lies on the floor, stained with something yellow, something red.

The sores are worse, but, as you turn, you think they're doing the job—the tape, that is. Your breasts are flat now, flat against your chest, covered in dark lines, rough bobbles from the cloth. They feel raw, but it's fine. It's all fine. No rattles, it's fine.

That's my girl, let it all out. Let it out.

ō

The bath is warm, your back hurts, but he is there with you, on the screen, in your arms looking away, so coy, so coy, such a gentleman. You rub the screen against your face, feel the fine hairs on your arms start to rise up, feel something stir down in the desert of scars, the nest of criss-crossing lines and hate. You slip a hand down your body, feel the curves coming back, filling with water while the chain rests cold from behind you, uncomfortable and growing stronger—thicker, courser, can smell the iron, feel the imperfections. Somewhere inside you, the anchor is reforming.

The flat is silent except for the sounds of downstairs arguing. Voices, a shrill then a low, then a thump and a shrill, then a thump and a thump and a thump and a thump and—

The sores around your chest burn with a heat, with a prickling that refuses to stop and the water has taken on a subtle colour, rose petals, a pink that might turn red. Red again. Who knows. It's warm for now, and the water is washing away the rest of the day. She can't stalk you here. She can't see you, can't look at you. You run a hand over your scalp, feeling the long hair there flow with your hands, follow them down your spine, your ribs, which stick free, the beginning of the metal...

I like a girl who knows how much to eat. I like a girl who looks good.

You touch the small cut on your scalp, let the single silver hair twist around your fingers, gentle and soft. Its roots have run deep, have wormed their way down, you can feel them tickling the back of your eyes. You let the hair slip gently over your fingers, then run your hand back over your scalp. Your hand catches in a knot of hair and you leave it tangled, pull down, feel the sharp pain on your scalp. You look over at him, at his slight smile, at the pixels which swim in the steam of the bath. You look at his hair, his short silver hair. You pull yours again, your long tendrils, thick with sticky water, clinging together, lashing down like a whip.

Wow, you look great! You should really put the effort in more often.

ō

The pills take the edge off, you remembered them finally, but the crying lasts long into the night, and only then the gin makes you feel less of it, or care less. Hard to tell. Pain, you see, you feel, pain pain pain. When you close your eyes, you still feel the anchor in your heart, the chain leading through your spine, wrapped around your chest, then pulling out the window and towards him. It pulses in the night, it pulses with his heartbeat when he runs, pulses with his movements as he yawns, pulses with his thrusting when he fucks her. Pulses when he kisses her, when she rides him whe—

The vomit is harsh and yellow, it burns all the way out and you realise you've done it on his side of the bed. He'll be mad, he'll be mad. He'll be mad! He'll—

You flinch, stop, realise he isn't coming, won't come and clench his—stop. You stop, take a minute to stare at it there then go to sleep, while he watches you from the frame on the other side of the room. And on the left wall. And on the dresser. And on the bedside table. And from the pillow. His eyes are gentle and grey. Grey like rainy days and gently padding around the house while he naps, getting his slippers ready, getting his drink ready for when he wakes. Padding around grey days, grey light, grey eyes. It lulls you like his passions, like his moments, like old memories. He's so good for you, he tells you, you know it. You know he doesn't want to hurt you. It's the only way you'll learn. The only way. It's not that it's just a cup you smashed, it's the principle, and now he'll get the whip, you deserve it, the knife, you knew it would happen, the fists, you shouldn't have told anyone. But you miss his skin, the way he kept eye contact, made you better. The thoughts are old, well worn like carpets, arguments, war wounds. Grey. It coddles you to sleep. You wake up on the floor again, running your hands through the shag carpet, ear to the floor, listening for his breathing, feeling the pulse and rattle of the chain as it jerks and stabs and whips.

That's my girl.

That's my girl.

ō

They're looking, they're all looking! You need to get out of here, you need to just get out of here right now, right quick. Someone touches your arm, you spin, face her.

"We have other brands, ma'am, if you'd l—"

"D—don't call me ma'am!" You scream, shrill, tears spill onto the floor.

For God's sake don't embarrass me! Just—just fuck off!

They kick you out of the shop, gently, but forcibly. How can they not have his brand? Or his shade? Or his scent?! How can they not have it! You need it.

You rub your eyes with the back of your hand.

For fuck's sake don't fidget, this is important to me. Sit up straight.

You rub them anyway, can't help it, the contacts don't sit well, but you need them. You look at yourself in the mirror, the cloth bindings already red in dimpled spots of open again wounds. You can see the threaded scars sticking out just above the pair of boxer shorts, worn now, smell only of you. The criss-cross scars stick out like weeds across your skin, stick out in straight lines, straight as a line, clean cuts for clean training. It's what you got for lying. You look back up at your chest, flat now, and your open hand, close your eyes and squirt the cream onto it. It's not his brand, the rebel thoughts scream, but you push them back. He must have changed. Must have, might have. You push back tears with a shuddering breath that pushes against the bindings, makes you wince and the chain rattle. The anchor shifts and stabs both lungs. Pain, pain, but no time. Don't embarrass him. You smear the shaving foam against your face slowly, savouring the popping feeling, the scrunchy foam so pleasant and soft, like him, like his eyes. You take his razor, which still smells of the bottom of his rubbish bins, but you can just imagine the smell anyway. You look at your face, at his face, then run the blade over his chin. You press down, take it slowly, in your head you hear the rasp of tiny hairs clipped, of the stubble chipped away, presented well to the world. You only cut yourself a few times, and only when you hear them arguing downstairs. You wonder if he still has the rod. You know he does. You clean the wounds, pretending your hands are his, moving them in the old familiar way, the way he used to when he was sorry, when he was gentle after the storm. Then you get ready.

I'm only doing this to help you. You know I don't like it when you make me do this to you.

You put on the suit, feel it crisp against your skin. The purple shirt, the dark red tie. You practice his side smile in the mirror. You practice his voice, poor parrot, but if you whisper you can fake it. The words tumble in your head like blows. You stare at the smashed cup, the death of love. You run your hands through the stubble of your hair, look at the grey light that bounces off the dye. You look at the grey contacts in your eyes, and realise it's almost time.

You spray yourself with the last of his scent, then throw the bottle against the mirror. It smashes. Glass rains down around you. Finally, you have his anger, but you keep your eyes closed, until the arguing from below stops.

There's no basement.

There's no basement.

The more you say it, the louder it gets, until you open his eyes and he stares at you, he's in front of you, angry, sweat on his hair, sweat on his face, the rod in his hand.

You deserve this, you—you fat pig.

Everything I did for you!

Where are you going!?

Get back here!

GET BACK HERE

You—

His head hits the mirror, where it was, the gap, the wall, the reflection that has stayed after the glass has fallen. His head hits the mirror as you grab it and throw it against it, again and again. His expression never changes, just that smile, just that smile, as you tire, as it hurts, as every smile kills you, destroys you. As every single crunch of the mirror sends more blood down his face. Until the smile is full of broken teeth, until the hair is red all over, until you can't slam him anymore.

I'm sorry, I'm sorry, I'm sorry—

You feel the smile stretch your lips till they split, your red raw screams all gone as you hit the floor and your phone runs out of battery.

HELP, MY DOG IS ISAAC NEWTON

Bill Plant woke up and sighed. He was sick to death of being Bill Plant. But no time for self-pity, he had a dog to walk. Since his wife died he'd struggled. It was the quiet, a seeping silence filled the neat house. His daughter came over most days and banged about in the kitchen but her noise was not the same. Bill had taken to talking to the dog but now there was something very amiss there too.

"Help, my dog is Isaac Newton," Bill Plant wanted to shout down the town centre. He wasn't mad, well not yet. He knew full well shouting would get him ignored by shoppers or worse patronised by the new bobby. But if enough people heard him on a busy Currys-Sale-Saturday, someone would come over. Quietly, like after the bobby had gone. Maybe put a brown hand on his arm and smile. They might introduce themselves, as so-and-so who had an uncle or aunty in-the-know at the new Hindu temple. Since Sue's death, news of the new Hindu temple had made quite a splash in the local rag. All plaster elephants and hysteria about traffic jams. There hadn't been any traffic jams on the day of the funeral. *God,* it was such an ordinary day. Bill had wanted a drama to mark his wife's passing. A giant jam of elephants, billowing saris and that pink powder they threw about. Anyway his thoughts began to digress. He wasn't a Hindu. He wasn't anything really, not anymore.

The dog, Isaac Newton (or should it be Sir Isaac?), was straining at his lead: keen to walk on, and Bill assumed, keen to ruminate upon physics. He had seen the dog, Sir Isaac, watching the Mars landing on telly. He wore an intense, involved look and wagged his tale. He growled when Bill's daughter hit the controls to watch more near-bollock-naked athletes powering round the Olympic Stadium. Bill set up a laptop so Sir Isaac had a continuous Mars news feed. This stopped the growling, but still the man was finding the whole situation quite a strain. Life had become unpredictable.

They headed towards the tatty park. It began to rain. Sir Isaac looked ahead and up at Bill and then ahead again as if to say, "Yes, we are finally going in the right direction." The rain got heavier and then slackened off, then got heavier again: typical London rain, annoying and inconsistent like his daughter's latest boyfriend.

At the park gateway, the gate had long since gone, Bill undid the lead. Sir Isaac ran straight up the hill. Bill clambered up after him. Feeling the strain in his knees and chest, he tried to organise his thoughts. Hell, if a dog could analyse so could he.

It all started when his wife died. His daughter befriended the pretty Indian girl next door. She began to change. She went to Zumba and swapped recipes: drop-scones for daal. The daal experiment, as Bill called it (when he was alone with Sir Isaac) had failed. Not a bit like the takeaway version. Man and dog shared a smirk.

There had been joss sticks, a trip to the temple, a festival. He cut his best roses for that, in silent thanks to their neighbour. She had sent a pan of her own daal round: thick, warm liquid, golden yellow with delicate flecks of garlic and red chilli. It was like tasting the afternoon sun. He even put down his scraped plate for Sir Isaac to lick. He was unsure if they had Indian takeaway in Sir Isaac's human life time. However the dog wanted more and barked at Bill's daughter as she washed the pan.

Bill's daughter had even borrowed a book on "Indian culture" she called it, from the library. She read it after tea, pointing bits out.

"Listen to this, Dad. It says reincarnation is…" and "Look at that photo," or, "Do you think Mum could come-back as…"

Bill would sigh and thump his newspaper down. "I'll walk the dog," was his reply. However, the more he heard, albeit only edited highlights, the more he came to believe in a slim possibility. The author, Gowri Shankar Balasubramanian, had done his research. Reincarnation was presented as a sensible explanation of many things Bill had wondered about recently.

On the annoying day he had to pay a hefty fine for the overdue reincarnation book, he noticed a large poster of Sir Isaac Newton above the library counter. He was struck by the resemblance between Newton and the dog: the long nose, the sceptical glance, and the dark eyes. On the spur of the moment he asked for a book on Newton, with pictures of course. Then later, discreetly at home, he put the book under the dog's nose. He wasn't sure what to expect, the dog was hardly going to quote the three laws of motion. However what the dog did do sent a chill down Bill's spine. The dog looked at the book, now open on the coffee table, and then looked at Bill. A sceptical look, as if he could not believe his owner had the wit to work out his secret burden. Bill leaned forward to turn the pages. The dog appeared to skim each page and then looked at Bill to turn over. And so the wondrous afternoon passed: man and dog engrossed. Bill apologised to Sir Isaac after a while. It was only a *local* library book, not a definitive edition of Newton's work.

The dog pushed his wet nose under Bill's hand as if to say, *Thank you anyway, I appreciate the gesture*. Bill noticed the dog wagged his tail more after this and he dreamt a great deal. Sometimes Bill noticed the dog looked sad in the quiet house. The long, empty days stretched ahead like a forgotten canal.

It must be tough being reincarnated as a colour-blind dog, Bill mused. Perhaps they should visit the vets. "My dog, well Sir Isaac here, is depressed. He can't see in colour and after his great work on optics," here Bill would show off his new expertise, "with prisms and rainbows, is there nothing that can be done? We're insured, could some lenses be made up?" Bill had half a mind to make an appointment but he couldn't really find the words to explain it all to his daughter. She would probably say Sir Isaac deserved what he got, that was a reason he came back as a dog and not something else that could see colour.

Bill wondered if he should just look the other way, for a quiet life. His dad was good at that. One time when his dad picked him after school, some older boys had pushed him into the road. They laughed as his dad braked abruptly. Stupid, crass 13-year-olds, full of it. Yet his dad said nothing. The boys ran off jeering. Billy (as he was known then), had been stunned. Yes the boys were intimidating to him, a first year, but he was only 11 after all. But *his dad*? The boys weren't thugs just prats looking for a cheap laugh. His dad could have taken them on, told them off. Billy remembered sitting in the car. It was very hot. He began to sweat in his cheap nylon blazer. His dad talked in a loud, hearty voice. Billy picked at this bag, chipping away at the Tipp-Ex tags Spider and Dean Dukes added during an anti-bullying assembly.

They stopped at a garage. Billy watched his dad flirt with the forecourt attendant, Fat Flora the Geezer Bird. "Twat," Billy thought. "I'm not having it anymore." Of course at this stage he wasn't sure what *it* was but after that he became a boy of quiet action. He chucked the Mars Bar away his dad bought from Fat Flora. He wrenched his bag away from Dean Dukes next lesson. As to the bullies: well let's just say when one of them "tripped" on the stairs, he took his mates with him. They weren't injured exactly, because as usual there was a stairwell crush. They fell on a couple of lanky mares who spilt Tizer on Deputy Dog's shiny suit. Deputy Dog, to give her credit, decided to tackle corridor *and* stair crushes after that. First years got to leave before the bell. They were in the canteen before the queues. Billy treated himself to banana milkshakes to celebrate and wondered if Napoleon (or some other general) ever wrote about little acts leading to big stuff.

So, with the taste of banana milkshake on his mind, Bill decided he and Sir Isaac would go out more, widen their horizons. He printed off some fake registered blind IDs, from some teenage website. They were Canadian which Bill explained to Sir Isaac was pukka. If anyone asked he could say in Canada they used mongrels as guide dogs, as they were more intelligent. With Bill's senior citizen pass they had been to almost 20 museums and several classical concerts, almost for free, though both became restless after an hour. One night they had even come back drunk after Bill realised pubs might be of historical interest to Sir Isaac.

At this time of day other dog owners were absent from the park, except the batty woman with blue hair. *Some species of FE lecturer,* Bill thought. They'd chatter occasionally about distemper and vets' fees. Blue-Tit hallooed her way towards him, blowing her nose in a giant paper towel. They tramped down the hill and sat out of the rain under the rotten wood of the Victorian bandstand. They smoked and talked and Bill found himself telling her about the library book on reincarnation. His theory unfolded, Blue-Tit was a good listener. She didn't interrupt unless she had to shout at her fat old dog and scoop up shit. He showed her a picture of Isaac Newton he'd photocopied at the library.

"Yes, yes," she said impatiently. "I know who Newton

is... or was..." Blue-Tit laughed knowingly, as if she used to date him. "You see I'm very intrigued by all this. I used to work with an Art Lecturer, before the cuts, who was convinced she had been a Potter in Previous Life. Now let me remember... She'd had a reading or been to some sort of Clairvoyant who was a Specialist in past lives... or was it a Medium... No," the woman continued, "it was a Hypnotherapist." Bill noticed how Blue-Tit sign-posted key words, a lifetime in FE he supposed. She frowned as the rain increased but showed no inclination to call her dog. "Of course it is all Very Well Accessing Our Past Lives with a Trained," Blue-Tit stressed the word "Hypnotherapist, but I've Never heard of anyone working with Dogs... imagine," she said warming to the theme, "Belle could have been Marie Antoinette."

They both gazed out across the park, Blue-Tit in wonder. Bill was as sceptical as Newton. Only if Marie Antoinette was known for farting continuously, he thought.

Bill felt Blue-Tit was only interested in *her* dog. He sighed. She heard the sigh and looked at him carefully. "You let me know what you find out. We could go together..."

"*What?*"

"To the Dog-Medium-Hypnotherapist person, have a Coffee after, make a Day of it..." she replied. She leaned forward, her giant bosom squeezed to a massive ball in her tight puffa jacket. Bill decided to go to the new temple instead. It would probably be free and less pretentious. He wouldn't tell Blue-Tit about it. Sir Isaac didn't like farting Belle either.

Later as he hung about by the park gateway waiting for Sir Isaac, he imagined a book-lined study and a man not unlike Mahatma Gandhi sitting on a desk telling him not to worry, everything would be all right. Gandhi would share anecdote after anecdote of such situations. Perhaps Bill would be introduced to other people. They would become friends, with a shared burden of grandiose pets. The youngsters could set up a website and reach out to others across the globe.

The dog returned panting and wet. He looked up at the man with a disappointed air, *Such a dim owner,* his eyes seemed to say. "Cheer up, Sir Isaac," Bill said too loudly, hating himself for his hearty tone. "One of these days you'll be reincarnated as..." His thoughts trailed off. *As what? As who?* Bill wasn't so cocky about predictions since Sue died. He changed tack. "If we hurry back we can get dry, grab a snack, Stephen Hawking's on the radio." Sir Isaac rolled his eyes and shook his head spraying dirty water on Bill's damp trousers. They trotted off together.

Life was as good as it was going to get, Bill decided. They would have to make the best of it, stressful though the changes had been. After all it could have been worse. His dog could have been Hitler.

AMATEURS, ALL OF YOU

And it rolled out in front of you, the silence. Right there, wedged between the procurator with his head in his hands and the officer with the wee ball of chewing gum rolled between his sticky white fingers. The clerk poised over his computer wondering what to type. The judge with a face like granite and her mind on lunch. What a moment. Considering an hour before I'd been sat miserable, staring at the dolphins stuck around the walls of the café. It was the way they looked out at you as you sipped your tea. Unnerving, all that sleek skin fading into the greying waves. Maybe it was just the paper that was fading. Either way, the kittens were even worse, sat there at jaunty angles in front of rainbows or a fucking meadow. You really couldn't make it up. Psychology was key though, crucial to the entire exercise. It was low-level stuff but it didn't matter. It was designed to get to you. I wasn't searched on the way in for some reason and I kept turning it over, turning it over in my head. It made you wince.

And now this. Someone tried to choke a laugh in the gallery. The judge stared harder and a boot went into somebody's shin. I smiled. It was hopeless, but you couldn't help it. Wee victories. All part of the game. The solicitor was really going for it. *Have you perhaps mistaken this courtroom for a classroom officer*, all that. Great stuff. The thing was, you couldn't really enjoy it. The theatre of it all. There were serious consequences at stake. But it wasn't that. It was the chairs. Too uncomfortable. I mean, really bad. And you were sat there for hours, for days, for *months* man, on those same chairs, not even able to say anything about it. You had time to notice these things. Time was the real killer.

Some functionary brought over a wastepaper basket. He was sweating in a cheap white shirt issued by some private security company headquartered in London. The funny thing was, it really did remind you of school. Such a limited environment, yet so many possibilities. This little white ball rested congealing on the copper's index finger and he curled it over the bin and tried to scrape it off with his thumb. It stuck to his nail. Desperate stuff. He looked over to the procurator and what a look it was. Real despair. He just sat there cross-legged at the bench rifling through his notes. Good luck getting any sympathy from him, I thought. You're drowning over there but good luck thinking he's going to stick out a hand for you. Prosecuting this pathetic material in the district while his friends are raking it in on conveyancing cases god knows where. Good luck to you. That's what I thought.

The poor bastard kept going. His free hand had been gripping the radio the whole time and he finally brought it into play, picking the offending object off his thumb and with a couple of flicks of the hand finally the bastard thing dropped into the bin. A real scumbag, I thought, making the whole thing so cheap. All you wanted was a bit of dignity brought to bear. For the paraphernalia of justice to impart some solemnity to proceedings as your life gets flushed down the swanny. That would have been nice. You'd have forgiven things better. You'd have understood it. I mean, at least you'd have been part of a tradition. But now instead the functionary is wheeling in a TV unit and you should have seen this thing. Like something you got at school. A monster, three levels, some old Panasonic that looked like it hadn't seen action for the best part of a decade, knocking through the doors of the courtroom, the wheels squealing as this eejit dragged it across the floor. This should be fun, I thought. At least that fucking copper is going to have to earn his bread now after his last performance. I didn't even recognise him.

You could never relax though. Some of them get to you. You tried your best to take control of the territory, nail your stake in the ground, search out the eyes of the lion and the unicorn, wear the crown, ignore the fucking thistles at the bottom. Of course the thistles were at the bottom. Some of them know what they're doing. They're not all daft. But you did your best, spring in your step, right attire, wee things like that. But we've entered the era of hostilities as I like to say and it's hard, it's hard work. Some of them get to you. There were two of them that really did. In the cells, that is. It's the wee things. No belt, for instance. You're holding up your jeans like you're incontinent or something. Really puts you off balance, no dignity. And the fact I had these daft socks on. When they came into the cell I was doing my best Camus impersonation, counting every wee mark on the wall, the desperate menshies carved under the window, the names, the cuts, remembering every wee thing and then trying to add another one. Didn't really work but at least I wasn't asleep or sat there like Genet, wanking away. One was a right smart dressed cunt, bald head, tie, tight face. But it was the other guy. Lanky, in a trackie top, casual as you like. Like he'd just headed over after coaching the under-twelves, was just stopping by on the way back home before his poor wife had dinner laid out for him on the table. No badge, no nothing. Just this big friendly face. Sent a shiver down your spine so it did.

And the next thing you know you're following them down this corridor, holding up your trousers, big toe sticking out from your big daft sock, thinking christ, I know Biko had it bad but I bet he got to do his last walk with a pair of shoes on. And before you know it you really are thinking about Biko because you're heading down a flight of stairs and it's quiet now and you clock the camera turned into the wall and two tape decks sitting there open and empty and two chairs but there's three of you, I know the game, it's no skin off my back, whatever you want officer, this seat'll do me fine. The tapes though, or their absence. That was the real killer.

When I was wee my old man had a cupboard full of them. The shelves stacked top to bottom, hundreds of the things, the track listings all hand-written, in pencil. You couldn't even see the ones at the top there were that many of them. He was a guitar man, that was what he did, played guitar, taught guitar, hadn't studied, hadn't nothing, but he played guitar like something else. And he'd dragged those tapes everywhere I guess and I learned the names, Dylan was his man, but all of them, Van Ronk, Bill Broonzy, Alex Harvey, and all those English ones, John Martyn, Grossman, Bert Jansch. We'd listen to them, I'd learn the names and we'd listen to them together, or at least they were always on, I always heard them, even when I was wee. Miles Davis, when I was really wee, and I always remembered that. And I'd sit and watch them argue, going at each other, in front of that cupboard with the door open and all the tapes, and think it was the music they were arguing about. I mean, like it was because one of them liked Blind Willie and the other liked Blind Blake and that was how they couldn't get on and they were so angry. It was daft but I really thought that.

Then one day she was gone and I opened the door and the tapes were all gone too and I knew that was really it. Looking up at the bare shelves, like all that music had just mysteriously floated off and it was quiet now, the shouting would stop and the music would stop too. And then later when I thought I'd worked out better what was going on, I stopped playing too, just to spite him. Like having Kafka there and not learning how to write. What an eejit. And then I'd ask him how his shelves weren't full of books, just those fucking tapes and he didn't even have those anymore. That that would really get to him, hurt him. But now I'm sat here in this room, and I can't play guitar, and I can't read, can't remember nothing, and there's no one I know in this whole world who can do anything as well as he can pick six silver strings. It just goes to show.

I'm sat in this chair anyway, giving it the no comment, and they're coming at me from all angles and meanwhile I'm thinking about these fucking tapes and it sounds easy but it's not. Like I said, there are certain things that get to you and they hit you with all sorts. We've nothing against you son, just a couple of names. So that's how you're playing it son, what about heroin, smack son, you'd tell us about that, and terrorism, wee weans getting their legs blasted off, know anything about that, or paedos son, wee kiddies getting done by some beast, you wouldn't no comment that would you now, oh you would, write that down, when asked if he knew about kiddies getting raped replied no comment see I told you he was a pest. And that big lanky cunt grinning away to himself and you couldn't even really be angry with him like he really was alright and he just wanted to get home. Thinking maybe his missus would sew up the hole in your sock and she was probably alright too. And all that just to get to a point where I'm looking at the judge sending some steroid-munching V-division animal away out to get batteries for the fucking remote control. Christ, it really does make you wonder sometimes. I gave my solicitor a wee close-lipped smile, for reassurance. You couldn't really be angry at her either, even though she went to the same fucking school as the PF and would no doubt be going for a coffee with her as soon as this was over.

That was another thing. The whole time you're sat there

you're thinking alright, you've got me now, but we won't all be in here forever sheltered by the grand tradition of British justice and its poorly paid security apparatus and this is a small city and I'll find you one day. And you're going through it all in your head. The revenge, I mean. Like when I was younger and working as a cleaner in a pharmacy up in the West End. Early starts but double time on a Sunday and it wasn't that bad pushing the old floss mop around and even doing the toilets and the staff canteen on a Monday. The good thing about being a cleaner is you really are the lowest of the low, you could be as miserable as you liked because everyone thought christ, I'm not doing great myself but at least I'm not the fucking cleaner. And it was liberating almost, a real sense of freedom. They'd search you on the way out to check you hadn't stolen any drugs or plasters or toothbrushes and you could get right resentful about it to them, how dare you question my integrity and so on. All you'd do is knock things off the shelves then sweep them up into a black bag and collect it from round the back later but still, they weren't to know. What right had they etcetera.

But this pharmacist, a right awkward one from Dublin, about as threatening as a wet tree, ruined it, this one wee saving grace, your right to be as miserable as you fucking liked. Pulling me up about the fact I didn't look happy in the job. Happy in the job! And I told him straight, I'm not happy in the job, the job is fucking shite and that's how I wasn't smiling and he could talk to my union rep if he had a problem. I never had a union rep but the line always seemed to work. But he kept asking me how I was, could I smile a wee bit more, or how I could help myself to biscuits from the canteen if that would help. I mean, real relentless stuff. So I'd go into work every morning and push around my mop and get right into it, turn up looking as fucked as possible, or drunk, or at least kidding I was drunk or that I was on the verge of a nervous breakdown, and stare hard into the eyes of the cashiers and the first couple of customers and try and make it as unpleasant as I possibly could. And think about what I would do when I ran into him. But in the end it was useless, absolutely useless. Six months after I'd walked I seen him with a group of pals, dentists or social workers, out celebrating a wedding or engagement or baby shower or whatever it was these people did. I turned round and he was there, his head bobbing about on the end of his long stringy neck and I fucking nodded at him. Nodded! And that was it. Bottled it. Absolutely useless. I mean, really. Absolutely useless. And it would be the same with this fiscal. I was bound to see him down the line, having brunch somewhere. I mean, it was almost a given. I was pretty much resigned to it. And I would probably say hullo. Jesus. At least I was prepared for the capitulation this time. I could take my time.

ō

The remote was working now. Small mercies. My solicitor kept pressing the stop button instead of pause and footage of the whole sorry day would have to be fast forwarded, unnecessarily by the way, in front of the judge and the coppers. Repeatedly. Just this endless loop. Although to be fair to them, they did look faintly embarrassed and I was in no position to dismiss any gesture of goodwill. The thing was, I knew as soon as I left the close that day that it would turn out badly. Now I'm no believer in fate but it was definitely a premonition of sorts, the sort that makes you question what it is you've set out to achieve. Not just on one particular day, but as a whole, on all the days, as it were. Just a wee thing, but significant nonetheless. A moment of hesitation and then a decision and then this feeling that somehow, in a way you couldn't quite sense, that something significant had taken place, and not in a good way, that you'd made the wrong decision and you knew it but you couldn't change it even if you wanted to, which of course you could, and you did, but you were set on this path now and that was all there was to it and it would end in something terrible. And it was only a simple choice. About what to wear, I mean.

I pulled on this green hoodie and that was it. I'm not one for sartorial deliberation. I'll wear the same thing for weeks, it's all the same to me. But for some reason that day I thought about it and that's what did it for me. The fact I actually stopped and faced it like a choice when what I should have done is accepted that there was no such choice, or not even that, but that the question didn't even present itself as such. I would have walked out the door and carried on as usual and it might not have seemed like much at the time but, it's hard to explain, a whole other city would have rolled out in front of me, a vision of light and tenderness working its way into the cracks of the pavements and the shop windows and the freezing air that made your lungs hurt and alive at the same time and everything could have been exactly the same and utterly different and the relentless noise of the trains and the traffic and the silence of the streets would have been like that freezing air in your lungs and not a choking fog you couldn't cough up or spit out for love nor money. And I searched for that transcendence in the scratched CCTV footage, on that old Panasonic, that was now being played over and over thanks to the almost indescribable ineptitude of professional members of the bar association.

And in all honesty I'd forgotten that footage existed and to see it, to have the chance to see it again, to look for that feeling in the smeared faces of the coppers and the witnesses streaming by, to try and catch my own face and my own dark eyes in that chaos and remember what it was like to feel, it was all too much, it was all too much, and I swear to god I started to cry. Right under the eyes of the judge and the procurator and the copper with his sticky fingers and the security guard in his sticky shirt and they thought I was joking, that I was making a mockery of justice and they lifted me right up out of the court and back down into the cells and there I thought about the next day and the day after that and if this would ever end.

CRAWL

MEET THE GOD-FEARING FAMILY MAN FEEDING THE POOR FROM AN ABANDONED LIVERPOOL ABATTOIR

By Thomas Jonally *City Centre* reporter

"It all started when the girls took over the men at work," John McCabe, 47, from Upton, Wirral, asserts in his poky office at the back of an abandoned city centre dockland abattoir. I am in Liverpool, where despite Turner Prize-winning streets and a European Capital of Culture title the city has over 200 people per day in desperate need of a food bank.

The stench of blood and sacrifice pervades the derelict building now trying to fill the mouths left hungry by the abolition of universal credit. I remind John of the government's responsibility but he is unconvinced, "Ok, yeah, the Tories have a part in this but believe me, I've seen it all, it was the women, they shouldn't have, you know... As my mum, god rest her soul, used to say, it's the women who keep the home happy. If there are no women at home what did they think was going to happen?" I don't respond so he continues, "My mum, she was always there for us, she made this." He points proudly at a meticulously stitched needlework which reads:

For I was hungry and you gave Me something to eat, I was thirsty and you gave Me something to drink, I was a stranger and you took Me in.

John grins. "Matthew 25:35."

I choose not to reveal my atheism but I can't help but wonder how a religious man such as John can reconcile his actions with the sentiment stitched by his mother.

John's food bank is the last remaining refuge for the hungry in Liverpool. In early 2021 the Conservative government abandoned various failed attempts to consolidate the porous benefit system into universal credit. With the continued rise of automation across the service industry and other low skill sectors many large UK cities such as Birmingham, Glasgow and Liverpool have struggled to keep their residents' heads above water. With the average house price in Liverpool now £255,000, more than ten times the average annual wage for a full time employee and with full time employment opportunities in steep decline since Britain left the European Union in 2019, John's food bank has become a lifeline for many of Liverpool's people.

It is certainly true that vulnerable people need food but surely there is a price too high to pay? John doesn't think so, "After the Tories blocked the supermarkets from giving us their left over bits and pieces and with no mums at home to cobble something together for them, I had to think of something, didn't I?" It was not only the legislation for the immediate incineration of retail food waste but also the application of anti-vagrancy laws to food parcel donations that rang the death knell for all the other food banks across the country. "I couldn't just let the poor buggers starve could I? Come on," John says with a glance at his watch, "It's almost feeding time."

I follow John from his office towards the enticing smell of Scouse simmering on a hob. In a makeshift kitchen two women bicker over whether the four huge pots of Scouse, beef stew to the uninitiated, need an extra sprinkle of salt. "This is my wife Jess," John says gesturing to the younger of the two who doesn't meet my eye as she shakes my hand. "And this is my Aunty Carol." Carol is a northern powerhouse matriarch who ends the salt debate with the clang of a lid. I am curious what the two make of John's endeavours, "He's like the Wirral's Bono!" Carol cackles, "But I'm a better singer," John says, they both laugh but Jess does not join in with the hilarity. "Do you want a bowl?" Carol asks gesturing to the steaming pans, I decline explaining I'm not hungry which shoots Carol's thin pencilled eyebrows up into her hairline, "No love, I meant do you want to feed someone?" Before I can reply John chips in, "Don't worry this one will be on us. Just you make sure you write us up fair."

After donations dried up John began a unique scheme. 'Clients' pay John to feed a bowl of Scouse to the 'Users' who queue around the block at 'feeding time.'

"At first," John explains, "I ran it as a Buy Someone A Lunch kind of thing. We charged a couple of quid for a bowl and that was ok for a bit but then even a couple of quid got too much. Then some fella came, bought a bowl and gave me a twenty quid note and said keep the change. We were made up but then, you know, he did what he did and I realised that whether anyone likes it or not this is the future of feeding the poor. People have to get something out of it too. No one wants to just give for giving sake anymore. Like I said, these fellas, their mums are out working, their wives, sisters. Sometimes earning more than them! They have to feel, you know, like men again." Now John charges clients £25 per bowl. I am interested how the profits are distributed, "Everything goes back into the business," So John does consider this a business? "Well, yes." But on his website there is a registered charity number so is John tax exempt? "You would have to ask my accountant," John smirks with a wink.

John leads me to a well decorated waiting room which is swarming with the low hum of excited chatter. Two teenagers, "Lovely girls," according to proud dad John, are distributing raffle tickets and as each number is called John takes payment and directs the 'Clients' to the kitchen. I try to engage with them but they ignore me. They are predominantly men, it looks like I have stumbled into a coven of middle management, creased white shirts, grey polyester trousers and primary coloured lanyards. They dismiss my questions with various accents, a few Scouse but most not. I hear the cities and towns of the UK, from Brummy to Cockney, Welsh to West Country. I join the queue to the kitchen behind one of the few female clients. Aunty Carol exchanges her raffle ticket for a steaming bowl of Scouse and Jess absently reaches for a raffle ticket then nearly drops the bowl when she recognises me. We both hesitate but when the man behind me grunts I snatch the wooden bowl from her hand and follow the herd to the outside courtyard.

I blink frantically in the transition from dim artificial light to bright afternoon sun. My eyes adjust and I see the courtyard is already full of scattered bowls and spilt stew. 'Users' who have entered the courtyard from an outside alley are crawling on their hands and knees trying to scoop as much of the scalding hot food into their mouths as possible. The woman before me sniggers as she pours the contents of her bowl into the outstretched palms of a young woman who has a little boy cowering at her ankles. The young woman sucks every morsel of meat dry then passes the flesh for the boy to chew, she does the same with every chunk of potato, sucks all the juice from them until they are gleaming white baby teeth which she slips into her jacket pocket. Across the courtyard most of the 'Clients' have their smartphones out, recording their donation for posterity. Capturing close ups of 'Users' poring over carrots and potatoes, trying to dust off the dirt but salvage the broth.

Gentle fingers tap my ankle. A gaunt middle-aged man peers hopefully up at my bowl. I glance around for a spoon, fork, anything but there are none. No one here expects cutlery. I squat down and try to hand him the bowl but he won't accept it. He is nervous, his eyes dart from my full bowl to the exit gate. A sharp kick to my elbow sends the bowl clattering to the ground. The man begins to eat. I turn to face Carol, she is furious, "If you're here you either do it properly or fuck off."

As I look around the courtyard at the relatively rich feeding the poor it is not the voice of God I hear. Instead, as the clunk of fallen bowls, the frantic shuffle of hungry feet and the relentless synthetic shutter clicks rise to a crescendo, it is the sound of my own screaming.

THE SUB-REGIONAL (INTERIM) UNIT MANAGER

Dennis sat wedged between plastic hand rests, anxiously pressing his thumbs onto the meeting agenda so hard that the ink transferred from page to skin. As a Sub-Regional (Interim) Unit Manager of five year's standing, he was summoned to the Annual General Meeting and in his capacity as new blood, he had spent the morning being assessed by twitchy head office colleagues as either a threat or irrelevance. He assumed, correctly, they had concluded the latter.

The G. A. Leonard company was founded in the late 18th Century, at first little more than a penny bazaar selling hats, scarves and discredited medical pamphlets in fledgling train stations throughout Great Britain. After the boom of steam powered transport and several generations of unpredictably capable descendants this became the GAL Corporation, floated on a dozen major stock markets, recognised as a household name and high street staple in the ubiquitous Hey GAL stores. They were not, on pain of litigation, to be referred to as just shops.

With an average of three or more branches in most towns and cities, they promoted each avalanche of business growth with full page advertisements in the pages of magazines aimed at readers with burning aspirations, and middling intellect. It was in just one of these publications that Dennis learned of the opportunity to *Be your own boss* ...and everyone else's, and *Stamp your personality on your stamp of authority,* and had applied, successfully, for one of their endless manager vacancies. The GAL Corp lawyers had drawn up human resource contract terms which had to be parsed through the Geneva Conventions at The Hague for permissibility, setting the probation period for new Sub-Regional Unit Managers at a minimum of 10 years. As such, Dennis was still saddled with the interim prefix to his current station, half a decade into the job.

Dennis was in the dying embers of his 29th year when he was recruited, the product of a second-class degree from a second-class establishment in a shapeless and vague academic discipline. He worked his way, straight out of university, half way up and all the way across the middle management of a tedious retail group, whose aim was to inject a profit margin into the short journey their products took from distant offshore factory to domestic landfill. Thousands toiled, like Dennis, through a 40-hour week in the trade of products so mundane that no one would ever conceive the input of live human beings in their creation. If a dinner party guest ever discovered their neighbour was employed to issue the purchase orders of say, personalised house-warming gifts in the shape of hearts or anything made from reclaimed timber, they might find themselves serving a custodial sentence for grievous bodily assault with a dessert fork. What little Dennis knew about dinner parties was enough to realise this, and he wanted out. He was attracted to the security and the autonomy promised at GAL Corp, a heady cocktail of creative freedom and viable pension options for any ambitious retail manager.

On Dennis's first day, he arrived at the shopfront 25 minutes early and turned the key, which had arrived the previous day by premium courier along with a thick welcome binder and a book of two-for-one cinema vouchers, lifting the motorised window shutter like a stage curtain on his new life. The staff arrived between 10 and 40 minutes later and Dennis decided to let the two sullen acne-carriers who shuffled in at 9:10am, eyes heavy from the effects of online gaming and cannabis resin, off the hook on this occasion, having read the chapter of his welcome binder on *Becoming a beloved leader* thoroughly over breakfast.

As the first year came and went, he felt the keen sprouts of professional rapport blooming with his staff and although he had to let one of the spotty kids go in the end, he was on first-name, birthday, and preferred-alcoholic-beverage terms with the whole team. Dennis resolved to further deepen this bond by encouraging his staff to express their individuality across the product displays, their sales technique, even their work attire. He shouldn't wonder that the regional managers would be impressed by this display of sub-regional initiative. He smiled assuredly walking home past the other two Hey GAL stores on that side of town, indistinguishable in their slavish adherence to window dressing guidelines.

Dennis's store was visited on an annual basis by a representative of head office, Shannon Mulgrave, who poked around the displays, tapped notes into a tablet and asked curt, ambiguous questions. Dennis was particularly irritated during her last visit when a group dressed in tentatively customised high school uniforms came in to browse and concluded the store layout was "totally mad" and "impossible to find anything". Each pronouncement, guarded from the judgement of peers, was said from behind a force field of sarcasm and interrogative inflections, before they trudged off to find another, more compliant, branch.

The afternoon session of the meeting began with intangible macroeconomic projections, which mostly passed Dennis by, as if the engineering blueprints for the Golden Gate Bridge were being explained to one of its iron bolts. The Associate Director of a department that had something to do with branding, but not marketing, stood by the podium to speak, wearing a suit with trousers which ceased well short of his sockless ankles, and a pair of cream espadrilles.

"It has been a banner year for the company," he said, beaming like a new parent or teatime quiz show victor. He presented a large Venn diagram, with all the flourish and theatricality one could muster for two interlocking circles fat with hideous jargon. They were encouraged to focus their attentions both inside and outside the company. Inside, and indeed outside, the physical stores. Inside, and of course outside, themselves. Dennis tried hard as he might but could only get within squinting distance of feeling any of it made sense.

He was followed by the Associate Director of Marketing (not Branding) who had retired from a successful acting career in television soaps, amid vague and legally embargoed accusations involving a Member of Parliament and a length of garden hose, to embark on a timely career in the private sector. Her keynote speech was as impenetrable as the last and Dennis was by now, on the ropes.

Another break was signalled. Dennis glanced to his left and right at the strangers he knew as colleagues sitting next to him. He smiled a weak hello to one side and offered a meek wave to the other.

"First timer?" said the man to the right. His handshake was firm and leathery, it seemed to Dennis that he was negotiating the transformation from abrupt and athletic in his younger years to a more considered and avuncular form. "Charlie Millbank, Sub-Regional for Stockton and Teesside, Unit 2," he said. Dennis found the delivery of name and rank quaint, thinking he must be from a military background. Territorials, not regular army. "First year for me since I lost the interim. Truth be told, I'm thinking about packing all this in. I've got a pal in Norfolk who runs an outward-bound centre, needs an instructor. Half of them are ex-servicemen like me, of course." The woman to Dennis's left turned swiftly away, not wanting to be party to such heresy as talk of early retirement. Dennis excused himself and queued for a cup of coffee, which when dispensed from the plunge-levered urn, was pungent, oily and lukewarm. Dennis added two sugars in a futile attempt to revive it.

As Dennis returned to his seat, a blizzard of excitable

whispers fell on the room and several groups of people, despite the comfortable temperature in the conference hall, were wearing padded gilets and rushing to tripods with long lens cameras. The ripple of anticipation grew closer.

"The Leonard family," said Charlie. "They show up every year but of course everyone acts with as much surprise as if The Beatles were getting back together. Including the dead ones."

Two brothers and one sister, the latest inheritors of the Leonard family fortune held minority control of the company, having been gifted senior company roles where they could throw their weight around at ceremonial events without impacting too much on stock value. Their parents died many years earlier when the family jet went down over the Atlantic, all three spared behind the walls of exclusive boarding schools. When the black box recorder was recovered, it contained a recording of Leonard Senior dictating an agenda for the next board meeting, barely audible over the sound of the decompressing cabin and Mrs Leonard's shrieks of terror. It had become one of those "where were you when you heard the news" moments in British culture, in Dennis's case, queueing in a garage to pay for a tank of diesel and a prawn salad sandwich which would give him food poisoning.

Archibald Leonard was the eldest. He was in the vanguard of society heirs who had stepped up the game from vintage port and backgammon evenings in each other's castles and townhouses to cocaine-fuelled rampages in city nightclubs, backstage passes at music festivals, and high-speed drag races the wrong way down the M1 at 2am, oftentimes driving irreplaceable masterpieces of automotive engineering, originally summoned by a head butler for master's appointments in town, only to end up skidding to a halt on their rooftops in a ditch near Hemel Hempstead. He was a tabloid favourite, sure to provide lines of copy by swinging punches, traffic cones and even a couple of girlfriends at swarming paparazzi, and more copy still at the subsequent trials. His role at company events was to trade off his rock star credentials, say absolutely nothing and refer requests for DNA proof of fatherhood to the company lawyers.

Less was known publicly about his brother Philip. He had been excluded from mainstream education as a five-year-old and had attended a self-styled school for the physically and mentally gifted, where he was the subject of a series of studies jointly funded by the school's founding philanthropists and the Ministry of Defence. The results have been sealed under the Official Secrets Act for no less than 80 years. He excelled in sport and devoted his efforts to mastering a series of obscure winter sports, dropped in succession by the International Olympic Committee due to lack of viable competition. He showed little aptitude for, and less interest in, business and suffered this annual family parade with much less good humour than that.

Betty Leonard, the youngest of the three, would not have tolerated her given name were it an abbreviation, but to her infinite distaste it was thus registered at birth and, during her mother's short-lived fascination with the Church of England, dedicated to the Lord accordingly. She felt the name, when spoken in full, was reminiscent of a witless flapper girl from the 1920s, or someone high up in the Women's Institute. She had a remarkable business mind and was often consulted by the Board of Directors, breaking the habit of an epoch, to advise on this direction or that. Her CV offered a glimpse into a baffling range of vocations. She had, in turn since her 16th birthday, found gainful employment as a sommelier in Marrakesh, a cage fighting instructor, a glass blower, political advisor to the Under-Secretary of State, a garlic farmer and reader in residence at the Shetland Library.

They arrived, and were met with a standing ovation, fanning out and filling the room like a gas leak. Dennis stood and matched his enthusiasm to the pitch of his most immediate colleagues, kicking over his coffee as he joined the appreciative foot-stamping. After several minutes of hysteria, everyone returned to their seats, some enduring the indignity of dabbing mascara-stained cheekbones or refastening the buttons on their shirts.

Archibald, his face obscured behind a pair of huge bug-eyed sunglasses, waved his appreciation to the floor and Philip looked at it. Betty stepped forward to the podium. "Thank you. Thank you all for being here with us today," she said as the sound engineer got to grips with her confident voice projection which caused the microphone to feedback. The first part of her speech covered another round of market reports, but she spoke with clarity, and Dennis was able to keep up, laughing without irony or dutiful compulsion at the interspersed jokes. The two brothers, either not following or not listening, took their cues from the room.

Betty Leonard continued. "Now one of the things we pride ourselves on at this company, is our consistency. Go into any store, anywhere, and you'll find the exact same pashmina scarf or mohair beret in the exact same part of the store as anywhere else." A chorus of eager murmurs sounded in agreement. "But wait, before you congratulate yourselves too much, remember that we must not be afraid to innovate, to change, to evolve. I chanced upon a routine inspection report of one of our sub-regional units on the flight over this morning, and I was impressed by what I read. I'd like to bring one of our bright young managers up here to introduce this. Dennis Lapwing, can you come up here? Are you here, Dennis?"

Dennis sent a gulp down his throat and seemed to feel himself sinking down with it. He expected his efforts to be recognised with a polite letter of commendation or a pat on the shoulder at a staff appraisal and was unprepared for such sudden and public acclaim. He rose to his feet, excusing himself as he wedged past fellow colleagues who in equal part admired, envied and wished for an imminent fatal accident to befall him.

"You're for it now," called Charlie after him with a wicked grin.

"Dennis," said Betty, seeing him emerge into the aisle, "come up here, join me at the front. Say hello to Dennis everyone." Everyone said hello, with a microscopic fraction of the enthusiasm they had shown the Leonards. "Why don't you tell us what you've been up to, I read your report with great interest." She gestured towards the podium. Dennis began to experience the condition of operating outside oneself the branding director had mentioned. He looked on, with serene equanimity, realising this brilliant woman had just made the most terrible mistake and that mistake, was him. He thought he could hear his own breath at a million decibels inside his skull, only to return from his reverie to find his breath was indeed amplified at considerable volume via the podium microphone he now stood a few inches away from.

"Hello," he started promisingly, "I'm Dennis. I think what Ms Leonard wants me to talk about is how I sort of, broke the rules," tailing off less so.

"Not just how, but why," she interjected.

"Um, I thought, it would be a change of pace. Something for the guys, the team, to get behind."

"A change of pace," repeated Betty, "something to get behind. This is all great stuff."

Dennis was quite sure it was not. "Go on," said Betty.

"Well, that's about it really. I let the staff move things around the shop to where they liked them, wear their own clothes to work, stuff like that. The team, they all seemed to like it," said Dennis.

"And the customers? Did they like it?" said Betty, as though angling for the big reveal in some dastardly murder mystery.

"Yeah," said Dennis, "Some of them."

Betty grimaced, like a conductor who had steered the orchestra to a poignant cadenza, only for the percussionist at the back to drop his big cymbals. She cut in. "Well, as I said to Steve all those years ago: people don't know what they want until they see it. He ripped that one off from me, the bastard, but I can't claim it back now he's gone to the big iCloud in the sky, can I? Look, I think Dennis here has really hit on something. We'll get nowhere offering up homogeneity, in perpetuity." Betty Leonard felt this was her best gag of the day, but it didn't get much of a laugh.

ō

It had been three months since the company meeting and Dennis lowered the shutter on his store window, the gleaming silver key that had arrived by courier now faded and featureless. GAL Corp had suffered a disastrous quarter, the impact of which was yet to be truly felt on the high street, although it had reached Sub-Regional Manager level that blanket closures were imminent. Betty Leonard had gone missing, Archibald had been drafted in but was even less use than feared. One of Philip's obscure sports had been renewed for the next Winter Olympics, so he was busy training with Team GB.

Dennis began his walk home, passing several Hey GAL stores. Betty Leonard said in her last press conference before she disappeared, not naming Dennis specifically, that one weak link can do all the damage. As he walked, he saw the shutters descend on one store after another, their window displays, in every detail and in uniformity, the same as they had ever been.

JAMBANJA

She gathered then shoved all the papers into a well-worn, brown leather briefcase. She would sort and separate them later at home, destroy some, particularly those with personal details. She was taking with her the ones with information that wasn't needed for open cases but could be used later and she was leaving behind those that did not have any sensitive information on them for someone from the main office to collect. It was safer she thought, to pack the ones she was taking with her in the check-in suitcase. Her hand luggage would only be the tablet and the two novels by Buchi Emecheta that she'd never had the time to read. She took one last look around the room. There was nothing much—just a small table and chair in the centre of the room, two tall, empty filing cabinets in a corner against the back wall and a bench along the other wall, just inside the door. Satisfied that all was as she wished it to be, she switched the light off.

An intense, opaque blackness immediately drowned everything. She closed the door behind her and stepped outside. For a few long minutes she lingered, holding on to the handle and accustoming her eyes to the darkness. She hated the few moments between turning the lights off and stepping into the deep black nights. She had always hated it. The sudden loss of sight always sent her into a momentary panic. She believed that the split instance of blindness gave other beings that had been in the darkness longer, an unfair advantage.

Her fear of the darkness was perhaps one of the reasons for her decision to leave. Every day, with each moment that the gloom approached and flooded the township, particularly during the cold months when it seemed that night fell so suddenly, she would find herself filled with nervous alertness. She would sit in the wooden cabin that was the office, distracted, and unsettled by sporadic bouts of energy. Her mind had always had the power to create horrifying scenarios of what could happen in the dark.

As the date of the election drew nearer, her imagination grew more vivid and the scenarios it spun, even more gruesome. This was not helped by the rumours, the reports and the evidence on her clients' bodies and in their troubled, sombre eyes. It was true that not all the beatings, the rapes, the torture and even the disappearances happened at night. It was just that she opened her office in the mornings. Also, if they came for her in the night, there would be no witnesses. She always thought that those who were arrested, or abducted during the day stood a better chance. Friends and relatives would carry placards and *toyi-toyi* on the streets demanding their return. Those who disappeared at night were often presumed to have fled to exile or chosen to go into hiding. She should have loved the darkness, felt invigorated and protected by it. Her work was best done under the cover of darkness, but she didn't know how to stop the constant torment in her mind. She would be happier once she got home.

A faint breeze carried the sweet, earthy promise of rain. The scent of gardenias wafted through all the other stale odours that were as familiar as the huge boulder at one end of the street. A permanent feature. Some stagnant water had collected in a ditch in the middle of the road, with rotting debris floating in it. Mounds of garbage dotted the roadside in front of the dwellings and a dog with a shattered skull and broken limbs lay decomposing at the street corner. All these revolting smells mingled with the aromas of different evening meals cooking on open fires behind the thousands of shacks that were the township. As if nature were playing a practical joke, a small forest of gardenia shrubs thrived just a few hundred metres away from where the carcass of the dog lay. The delicate, white flowers stood out obscenely amidst the drabness of the township but at a respectful enough distance as if even they sensed that life in the township was short and cheap.

Next week it would be a cat, a different ditch with different remains in it or mounds of rubbish at different roadside spots, but as she stood there she was convinced that in all the time she had been here, this township had had the same rank smell of deprivation and an ever-present air of anticipation and danger.

Another permanent feature were the urchins that spent their days kicking a plastic football about on the dusty streets until sunset when they would all disappear suddenly. Once the sun went down, the people of the township would stay inside, not venturing outside. They were not afraid of the dark. They were used to the dark and, unlike her, they spent most of their evenings in darkness. Although she called the cluster of dwellings a township, it was in reality an informal settlement—a shanty town. No official services. The dwellings were just a collection of shacks made of cardboard, scrap wood, rocks and scraps of sheeting on the outskirts of a sprawling city. The people knew how to survive without electricity but they also knew that bad things happened to people after nightfall, especially with elections so near.

The street was completely deserted.

She took a deep breath, wondering if she would miss it all—the smells, the silence, the noises, the filth. She wondered if she would miss the people, now her friends, mostly. Would she miss the worlds that the surreptitious notes and the people opened up—at once dangerous, distressing, rebellious but life affirming?

She enjoyed her work in the township, if enjoyment was an appropriate description. She was not under pressure to prove herself to anyone. Her work could not be openly acknowledged or hailed—not by the organisation that funded the work; not by the people that benefited from it; and certainly not by the government. She knew that this made it more unsafe. It was work that no one but the state should have been doing and yet, if they did, it would confirm that bad things were happening and the government didn't want to acknowledge that. The organisations that worked to pick up the pieces, like the one she worked for, could not own up to doing so for fear of victimisation, and the people that benefited from the work kept it quiet, to protect their benefactors. But the people trusted her and didn't ask too many questions. Everyone knew what had happened to her in the last place she worked but out of respect, they pretended they didn't. To them she was a legal advisor, a teacher, a counsellor, sometimes even a doctor and a lot of other things too; which made it worthwhile. She had tried to keep her work as neutral as possible. She didn't ask people about their political views or how they obtained the cuts on their hands or bruises on their bodies or why they wanted to get rid of the baby they were carrying. Her work was not to judge or give moral advice. Hers was to give them the assistance they needed—reference letters to doctors who would help without asking too many questions, transport and recommendation letters to safe houses and organisations that could provide counselling services, giving out food packets and other provisions whenever there were any and importantly taking pictures of all the injuries, and cataloguing them carefully, just in case.

However, as she stood in that street listening to the silence amidst the musty stench, she knew she would not be coming back to this office or into these people's lives again. They didn't know it. She imagined that they would turn up in the morning as usual. First the men, they were always first, and then the women and children—hungry, broken; and then she imagined they would just walk away again once they realised she wasn't there and would probably return for a few following days. They might wonder if she had been arrested, or killed, or whether she had become one of the disappeared. After a few days they would get used to the idea that she wasn't coming back. They would be disappointed, even sad, she liked to think. She knew that the office might find someonc to replace her or that a different organisation might come along, use the same small workplace amongst the smell of decaying dogs, fermenting rubbish and gardenias to do similar work, and that there might even be another woman they would call auntie so-and-so but, if none of that happened, the people would still get used to the disappointment because disappointment was another part of their lives. That's what life had become for these people. They couldn't even vote.

She felt that something momentous was imminent, and she wanted to be home when whatever was going to happen, happened.

She decided to take a taxi home. She felt a strong urge to walk down Sobikwa Street, just this last time to savour the mysterious quality of the night and, just this once, to face her fears and dare the night. She knew this was not a good idea. A woman doesn't take a solitary walk at night in a place like this. She'd never done it before.

She peered down the road and started walking. She would flag down a taxi at the end of the road, just next to the decomposing dog. She had toyed with the idea of burying it when it first appeared but she remembered her previous colleague advising her that if no one asked her to do something, she shouldn't. Someone would know who the owner was, who had killed it and why. There would be people who wished they could bury it—people whose children played at the street corner, people who loved animals and would have been appalled at the cruelty. None of them had buried it or buried other dead dogs or cats before this one and none of them would bury the ones after. She left it where it lay with maggots wriggling in and out of its orifices.

The thought of the dog's stench was too much and she made for the next street. Just as she was about to turn a boy emerged from the intense blackness of an alley, handed her a piece of paper, and slipped back into the night as suddenly as he had appeared. It happened so quickly that she didn't get a chance to ask. She considered just walking on to get her taxi and tossing the piece of paper on the ground but curiosity got the better of her. There was also the possibility that someone might be in trouble and needed help. She would read it, and then get her taxi.

Rather than walk back to unlock the office door and endure another terrifying few seconds of blindness when she turned the light on, she decided to continue to the street corner where she could read the note in the glow of a distant tower light. She read the three words, '*Chabvondoka! Jambanja Tonight*'

She turned the crumpled piece of paper, torn off from the corner of a mealie meal bag, hoping for more clues. If it had been day time she would have walked to the school teacher's house. In the three years she had worked in the township the school teacher had clarified numerous similar sorts of messages and smoothed over a few awkward episodes caused by her initial arrogance in thinking that she could learn all the ways of a people, in a few weeks.

She relied on information supplied in this manner to know where and when things would be happening but as with other local slang words in similar crumpled and hastily scribbled notes, she was not sure what *'chabvondoka'* meant in this case. Did it mean that the police or the army were coming in the night to carry out raids on suspected *enemies of the state?* Was it the ruling party supporters who were coming to terrorise suspected opposition party supporters? Sometimes there were revenge attacks. She wished it meant the people themselves were organising some sort of action.

The note was not signed.

She would go home and let someone else deal with whatever this was about she decided, but maybe the same boy was following her, expecting a reply.

"I know where they want you, auntie Maria," he said softly before starting to walk away. She didn't feel assured that the boy knew her name and that she couldn't see his face but she derived some comfort from the 'auntie'. She knew she had to go with him. She hesitated for a few seconds but her indecision did not last long. For if she tarried too long, the boy's form would blend into shadows and she would have to stumble in the darkness by herself. Was it morbid curiosity, dedication to her work or just fear? Maybe it was all three. She found herself tentatively following this boy through narrow streets and back alleys into the cool darkness of the summer night. The shacks always looked drab enough in the sun, but the darkness gave them a quality of musty poverty and squalor. They stood indistinguishable in the gloom. She would not be able to find her way back on her own. Heart pounding, she quickened her step.

She should have been walking away from all this, not faltering deeper into the seemingly unending cycle of destitution and despair and the ever-present threat of danger.

IDENTITY

The gaslight spluttered. Kate stared into the pocket mirror. Red hair, unconventionally short, sprang around her pale features. She'd kept her chin up, at least until he'd left the room. The wardrobe mistress bustled in. Furrowed brow. Seemed she had something to say. She rearranged the bad smelling costumes on the rail, cast a glance her way as she left, and said:

"It's half an hour, you know that."

Kate nodded.

She was alone again. Giggling and gargling came through the thin partition wall from the chorus dressing room next door. They knew what it was like to be part of the gang, the company family, and spirits were high. Kate was in a lead role which meant she couldn't be one of them. To be part of something bigger than herself, she had been tantalisingly close to that. An identity that was separate from her family circle. To have an identity unlinked to a father or a brother. She had heard other women talking about it. Heard there was nothing like it.

He hadn't had the guts to fire her straight away. The audience was already through the doors. In the bar. Buying programmes. But he hadn't been able to wait until after the performance. He was too angry. She had no doubt who would be her replacement. No doubt at all. Ada's growing confidence had little to do with her acting classes. Her dainty debut as a walk-on, was only a month ago.

She'd only just sent off last week's wages to her aunts, so now she would be short. Worse than that, it meant she was in debt. The costume could only be hired on a weekly basis, but he'd only given her one performance's notice. Only women in the cast had to hire their own costumes. After all, women weren't breadwinners, were they?

As Kate had dragged herself from the cobbles, blouse ripped and hanging out of her skirt, her hat long gone and her hair vibrantly on display, she thought she'd done well to elude the grasp of the policeman. It's just that she hadn't noticed the photographer.

Some people said being an actress was akin to being a prostitute. Some people saw being a suffragette, as something even worse. Something dangerous, unfeminine, subhuman. No longer deserving of courtesy, consideration or even means of earning a living. So she'd kept her interest secret.

She'd been brought up with middle class ideals. There was simply no requirement to be educated. As a woman, your destiny was to marry and breed. If that didn't pan out, you would look after your father until he died. So if your father died when you were a child, as hers had, marriage was a necessity. Who was going to marry a suffragette? Nobody would even employ one, not even a theatre. Afraid it would scare the audience.

Kate's aunts who had brought her up since she was ten, depended upon her making a living. To entertain them, she had fibbed. She told them of her fictitious involvement in the Movement. She waved away their flurries of concerns explaining that her work for the suffrage amounted to little more than stuffing envelopes. They would no longer believe that when they saw the picture on the front of the Times. Battered to the ground at the feet of a policeman.

Yet she herself had committed no violence, no crime. It was the first time she had come anywhere near the action. She'd been careful to stand off the pavement even—in the road. If you weren't on the pavement, she had read, you could not be arrested for causing an obstruction. But as the crowd surged, as it was pushed back by the police on their horses, she became surrounded by women fighting off the men in uniform, engulfed by them, mistaken for the same.

From where she stood, violence was surely not the way. Smashing windows, bombing buildings, setting fire to post boxes, Kate couldn't make the connection. Why was this going to change the law? However, she understood now that decades of talking had made no difference. In fact talking was just thrown back in the women's faces. The subject grew stale in Parliament, was removed from agendas, became the target of cartoons in national newspapers. As the years dragged on with one political trick after another, party politics taking precedence over natural justice, she grew to empathise with the rising frustration.

She went to see Annie Besant speak at the Royal Albert Hall. Kate crept into the Hall and slipped into a seat not really feeling that she belonged. She gazed at the radiant faces around her. There was a glow… what was it? Exuberance, could it be? Annie, the one-time leader of the Match Girls' Strike of a different century took the stage. Elderly now, she spoke still as a firebrand. Six months hard labour for breaking glass? Why weren't wife beaters punished as heavily as that! Surely, when the law is as dishonourable as that, as one-sided, as repressive as that, a lawbreaker fighting in the name of honour and freedom should be exalted. Kate found herself part of the communal intake of breath, she shared the upsurge in spirit, confidence and energy.

Men got their way with aggression. Just look at Ireland. It seemed that in order to make an impression on the men in power, women had to ape their behaviour. When the women did that, they were called "hooligan" and "hysterical". Kate looked around her. She didn't see rough behaviour. She didn't see anybody out of control. She saw plucky, determined, admirable women. She saw commitment. When she'd left the Royal Albert Hall, Annie's final words were singing in her head:

"Better remain silent, better not even think, if you are not prepared to act."

Not possessing any special talent, she had needed to find a way of protest, something perhaps she could quietly do on her own, that meant she kept her livelihood too. Her first step on this path was choosing to go and observe the protesters outside the Houses of Parliament. Now her job was in jeopardy. Realistically, gone.

What was the point? Where had this careful path got

her? Her face was now on display alongside the others at Scotland Yard. She didn't know what that might now mean. Would the police come to find her? Then court, trial, Holloway?

The wardrobe mistress swept into the room expecting to merely complete the finishing touches. She stopped short. Angry.

"Curtain's up in 15 minutes!"

Grumbling, the wardrobe mistress buttoned her roughly into the heavy brocade dress and tugged her wig grimly onto her head. It was too tight.

"Well, you've made your bed now, haven't you."

So she knew then. Did they all know? Would she ever get another job? She would probably lose her digs when she got back after the show. Her distinctive features that had given her a living in the theatre was now instrumental in her downfall.

She walked to the wings. As the curtain raised to audience applause, she waited by the sword that was in position for Act Two. He was plum in the sweet spot. Talking. His beloved monologue, centre stage, with spotlight on him. The audiences' faces in the first few rows glowed dimly from their seats. They were captivated by him. Engrossed.

This was the first time and the last time then. With a deep breath, she strode on to the stage and stood in front of him, blocking him from his audience. Releasing her unruly, shocking, glorious hair from the restrictions of the wig, she raised it above her head and summoned a voice from the very centre of her body:

"Votes for Women!"

As she turned, she saw his face screwed in anger, and his fist heading towards her. Her ear exploded as his fist connected with the side of her face. But she was already moving, fast, toward the Venetian backdrop. She flung the wig aside. With both hands she secured the hilt of the sword she'd brought on with her. Bringing it over her shoulder and with all her might, she split the Bridge of Sighs completely in half. The material was old. It parted like butter to a knife.

His full weight thundered towards her. The collision knocked all the breath out of her as they both barrelled through the backdrop, its final threads giving up with a groan. The sword shattered. It too had had its day.

"Shut your mouth!" He screamed into her face, his hand squeezing her neck, choking her against the wooden floor. Stage assistants scrabbled quickly forward and pulled him from her. They held him back and stared at her, mute with fright. "You shut your mouth" he gasped again, fury making him now incapable of any other words.

Iron pasted the inside of her mouth, her blood spluttered out onto the top half of that brocade costume. Hazily, she sat up and saw some movement in the audience, maybe a woman standing. From a muggy fog, her hearing suddenly cleared.

"Votes for Women!"

From the audience. In the stalls! Shouts, just a few, female voices.

"We want the Vote!"

"When will women—"

Kate saw one woman, silenced by her embarrassed male companion, jerked out of her seat no doubt to start an early and silent return journey home. Another two women were being escorted out by the front of house manager. One twisted her head and smiled at Kate. A triumphant, wonderfully wicked, smile.

It hit her system like a drug.

Solidarity.

THE AUTHORS

ANDY WARMINGTON lives and works in Northern Ireland with his wife Amy and young son Finn. Andy currently works at the Verbal Arts Centre in Derry, and was lucky to work with some fantastic charities, artists and diverse communities in the North East of England before that. He plays guitar and trumpet, at least until he's begged to stop, and co-hosts a podcast about whisky and music. Andy has been writing seriously for a couple of years. He is attracted to the rhythm of language and stories that cut through the mundane and ephemeral.

ELISA WEBB took an MA in Creative Writing because she had to 'make stuff' on the course not just go to lectures and write essays. This led to a debut novel *Darkling Park* (Patrician Press Halloween 2016) and a part-time Southern Gothic Imaginative Writing practice-based PhD at Kingston University.

ETHEL MAQEDA is a Zimbabwean short-story writer, based in Sheffield. She has some short stories published in various publications including in various volumes of the University of Sheffield's creative writing journal, *Route 57*: *Verse Matters* (Valley Press, 2017) and *Wretched Strangers*: *Transnational Poetry* (Boiler House Press, 2018).

D I SOUTHWARD is a novelist, teacher, and literary scholar. Currently living in Sheffield, he spends his time writing about reading and reading about writing. His work examines the way in which horror and the Gothic invade the everyday, and the ways in which we self-mythologise our own lives.

JENNIFER HAYASHI DANNS is a Scouse writer who divides her time between Liverpool, UK and Fukuoka, Japan. She is a graduate of Faber Academy and published a non-fiction feminist book called *Stripped: The Bare Reality of Lap Dancing*. Jennifer is currently working on a speculative novel called *The Mu* which explores the origin of gender roles.

JOEY SIMONS has lived in Glasgow for nearly his entire life. Over the last few years Joey has worked with the arts space Platform in Easterhouse to recover the radical political and cultural history of the scheme, through research, exhibitions and public talks. As part of this work Joey has produced a script for a play, and he's currently putting together a publication around the life and work of the Irish poet Freddy Anderson. Joey works full-time as an ESL teacher and he's an active member of the tenants' union Living Rent. He has been writing fiction for the past year and is working on several other group projects, including a territorial inquiry into gentrification, a community photography workshop in Govanhill and a project around Tillie Olsen's *Silences* and her alternative reading lists.

JOSH KING is a writer and illustrator living in London. He received his MFA in Creative Writing from Adelphi University, New York. His short stories have appeared in BlazeVOX magazine, The Matador Review, and The Year's Best Weird Fiction anthology. His nonfiction appears regularly in Texas' Newfound Journal. Josh focuses mostly on sensationalism and the speculative in his writing, and often finds its way towards pieces about obsessive religious groups or death-obsessed cults. His short story *The*

Anteater was nominated for the Shirley Jackson Award for speculative fiction.

LESLEY STRACHAN is the Arts Editor and a Director for Wandsworth Radio. For three years, she was a Trustee at the Curve Theatre in Leicester and is currently Trustee for the National Centre for Circus Arts in London. Lesley has directed a wide range of classic and twentieth century plays on the London Fringe, but since 2008 has mostly concentrated on published work of contemporary writers. The research she undertook when directing *Her Naked Skin* by Rebecca Lenkiewicz at the Bridewell Theatre in Central London, first ignited her interest in the women's suffrage movement. *Sylvia* was her first radio play about the internal strife within the Pankhurst family as they followed their separate paths in the battle for the Vote. It is available on Made in Manchester's subscription audio channel, Distinct from October 2018. *Identity* is Lesley's first published short story.

PAUL BROWNSEY lives in Bearsden, Scotland, and is a former lecturer in philosophy at Glasgow University. He has published around 80 stories in the UK and North America. His book, *His Steadfast Love and Other Stories*, is published by Lethe Press, New Jersey, USA, received a starred review in Publishers Weekly, and was a finalist in the Lambda Literary Awards. In trying to write stories he has found the biggest task to be to slough off his academic training, according to which everything must be spelled out on the surface, and to try to use words in such a way that the gaps between them speak.

RAJEEV CHAKRABARTI is a writer from Kolkata, India. He grew up in India and graduated from Delhi University's St Stephen's College. He attended graduate school at Boston University, and worked in the US before returning home to India. *Gargoyle* is his first published work of fiction.

SHYAMA KASINATHAN has always been passionate about books and has been writing since she was a teenager; starting off with terribly earnest poetry, before moving onto fiction. She took part in the Penguin Random House WriteNow event in 2017 and is a keen writer and blogger. She is currently seeking representation for a novel she has written for young adults. She lives in South West London, has two young children and works, part-time, in a University library.

THANK YOU

Thank you, yes you—the reader! We're really excited that you've bought and read our very first publication. We hope you enjoyed it and, if so, as the old mantra goes 'sharing is caring' so make sure you pass it on.

Great to have you with us!

THE MARGŌ COLLECTIVE TEAM

JOIN THE COMMUNITY: @MARGOCLLCTV

MARGŌ /ˈMAR.GO:/

FROM LATIN: BORDER, MARGIN, EDGE

MARGŌ COLLECTIVE WAS BORN OUT OF ADDICTION. ADDICTION TO GOOD STORYTELLING. OUR AIM IS TO EMPOWER WRITERS WHO HAVE BEEN PUSHED TO THE MARGINS BY THE MAINSTREAM AND WHO, LIKE US, THRIVE ON STORIES THAT WRENCH THE HEART AND PUNCH THE GUT.

WE ARE DRAWN TO STORIES THAT MOVE US TO TEARS, TO LAUGHTER, TO CHECKING THERE'S NO ONE LURKING BEHIND THE DOOR. COMPELLING CHARACTERS DRIVE GOOD FICTION AND MORE OFTEN THAN NOT WE PREFER THEIR COMPANY TO REAL PEOPLE.

MARGŌ IS AS MUCH ABOUT THE READERS AS IT IS THE WRITERS. WE'RE PASSIONATE ABOUT BUILDING A COMMUNITY OF PEOPLE WHO REJECT THE AUTOPILOT WORLD AND SEEK NARRATIVE ESCAPISM. WE'LL BE BRINGING STORIES FROM THE EDGES, STORIES FROM EMERGING WRITERS AND THE UNTOLD.

MARGOCOLLECTIVE.COM
HELLO@MARGOCOLLECTIVE.COM
@MARGOCLLCTV